the little death

michael nava

alyson books
los angeles | new york

I wish to thank Paul Gillette, without whom
I would not have finished this book,
and the Wednesday Night regulars—*in vino veritas*.

THIS TRADE PAPERBACK ORIGINAL IS PUBLISHED BY ALYSON PUBLICATIONS,
P.O. BOX 4371, LOS ANGELES, CA 90078-4371.
DISTRIBUTION IN THE UNITED KINGDOM BY
TURNAROUND PUBLISHER SERVICES LTD.,
UNIT 3, OLYMPIA TRADING ESTATE, COBURG ROAD, WOOD GREEN,
LONDON N22 6TZ ENGLAND.

FIRST EDITION PUBLISHED BY ALYSON BOOKS: MAY 1986
SECOND EDITION: AUGUST 1997
THIRD EDITION (15TH ANNIVERSARY EDITION): APRIL 2001

01 02 03 04 05 **a** 10 9 8 7 6 5 4 3 2 1

ISBN 1-55583-694-1
(PREVIOUSLY PUBLISHED WITH ISBN 1-55583-388-8.)

COVER ILLUSTRATION AND DESIGN BY MATT SAMS.

For Bill

Preface to the 15th Anniversary Edition

I began writing *The Little Death* in the summer of 1980, just after I had graduated from law school at Stanford and while I was studying for the bar exam. I was working at the Palo Alto, Calif., jail, located, like the jail in the novel, in the basement of the courthouse. My job was to interview arrestees after they were booked to determine whether they should be released on their own recognizance or held overnight until a judge could set bail. My hours were from 10 P.M. to 6 A.M. Palo Alto is an affluent university town without much serious crime, and often my only clients were a couple of drunk drivers or an inept burglar or an unfortunate prostitute. I had a lot of time on my hands. The cops who ran the jail had little use for someone whose job was to release prisoners, and they scorned my attempts to fraternize.

Inevitably, I found myself at my desk in the corner of a small room with a pile of legal outlines in front of me and the bar exam breathing down my neck. After three years of law school, however, I was unable to motivate myself to study the rule against perpetuities, the 18 exceptions to the hearsay rule, or the ins and outs of the ex post facto clause. I started, at some point, simply to write descriptions of what I saw and heard at the jails. Those descriptions eventually coalesced into the beginnings of the story that would become this book.

This kind of literary doodling was a habit so deeply ingrained in me that I did it almost unconsciously. I composed my first poem when I was 8 years old. By the time I was 12 I was writing almost every day, releasing onto the page all the words I dared not say aloud about the discovery of my homosexuality. Poetry was the form of my first work because poetry is a coded language and it suited my purposes; I could convey my anguished teenage emotional state without specifying its cause.

I came out when I was 17, and I gradually accustomed myself to this mysterious difference that seemed to set me apart from most people. As I did, I doodled less in verse and more in prose, and I began to think maybe being homosexual was a subject worth writing about. By the time I began the jottings that became this book, I was 24, in a relationship (with a lovely man named Bill Weinberger, to whom this book is dedicated), and out to everyone who mattered to me. When I got serious about turning my notes into a novel, there was no question in my mind that the still-nameless narrator would be an openly gay man.

But why a mystery instead of the usual semiautobiographical first novel? This had to do with the time and my temperament. In the late '70s, the landscape of gay fiction, such as it was, was dominated by a group of New York writers whose books depicted the hermetic world of the homosexual demimonde of Manhattan. Although billed as "post-Stonewall" writers, they were, in fact, a generation older than those of us who actually came of age in the late '70s, and the attitudes and assumptions that prevailed in their novels were distinctly unliberated. There was precious little difference between the doomed queens in Andrew Holleran's 1978 *Dancer From the Dance* and the doomed hustler in John Rechy's 1963 *City of Night*; they were all equally self-loathing, sexually compulsive, and morally irresponsible.

I failed to recognize anything on the pages of Holleran's book, or the works of Edmund White or Larry Kramer, that bore the remotest resemblance to my life. I was gay, true, but I was also a third-generation Californian from a working-class Mexican-American family, upwardly mobile but morally serious; determined to make for myself a better place in the world than I had been born into but without compromising my ideals. I was not tormented about being homosexual, and I knew what I wanted from being gay—not erotic adventures but love, a partner, a shared life. I was looking for a way to live in the world, not a gay ghetto in which to hide away from it, and in this pursuit not one of the fashionable gay writers—ghetto dwellers to a man—was of any use to me.

I had stumbled across only one writer, Joseph Hansen, who had created a gay character who lived in the larger world with courage, if not ease. Beginning with 1970's *Fadeout*, Hansen had written a series of mysteries featuring an insurance investigator named David Brandstetter. Brandstetter was not only openly gay but calmly masculine, competent at his work, compassionate even toward those who reviled him, and a romantic. He was altogether an admirable hero, and his creator, Hansen, was a superlative writer who, as an added bonus, wrote about California with as deep a love for the place as I felt. Hansen's novels also showed me that the mystery could broach large questions of morality and justice and paint a broad canvas of contemporary life. I also thought that writing a mystery would help me overcome the great stumbling block of all first-time novelists: creating a plot. Writing *The Little Death*, I learned the rudiments of my craft in a way I might never have if I had tried to write a book closer to my actual life.

It took me four years to finish the book. By then Bill and I had moved to Los Angeles, where I worked as a prosecutor. Bits and pieces of that experience worked their way into the novel, and somewhere along the line my nameless narrator acquired a name, Henry Rios. I also found a writers' workshop run by a man named Paul Gillette, a marvelous teacher of great generosity and no pretensions who shepherded me through the final draft. The book was completed in August 1984. Thirteen publishers rejected it before Sasha Alyson enthusiastically accepted it. The book did well enough that Sasha asked for a sequel. I had never intended to start a series, but I was still interested in the character and the possibilities of crime fiction, so I obliged him with *Goldenboy* and thus became a full-fledged mystery writer.

My career as a mystery writer was inadvertent, but my association with Rios over the next 17 years proved to be one of my more enduring relationships. Quite without design, I ended up chronicling the life of a man not unrepresentative of my generation of gay men. In the process I may have also written a kind of spiritual autobiography.

Michael Nava
San Francisco
March 2001

The Linden Family Tree

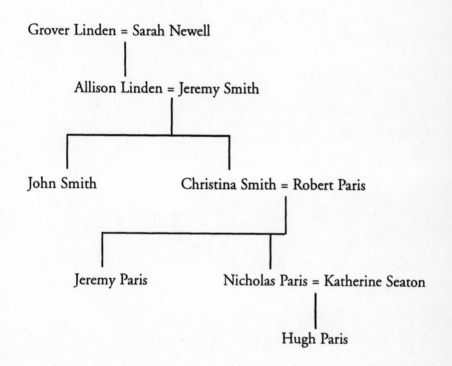

Grover Linden = Sarah Newell
|
Allison Linden = Jeremy Smith
|
John Smith   Christina Smith = Robert Paris
|
Jeremy Paris   Nicholas Paris = Katherine Seaton
|
Hugh Paris

— 1 —

I stood in the sally port while the steel door rolled back with a clang and then I stepped through into the jail. A sign on the wall ordered the prisoners to proceed no further; more to the point, the word STOP was scrawled beneath the printed message. I stopped and looked up at the mirror above the sign where I saw a slender dark-haired man in a wrinkled seersucker suit, myself. As I adjusted the knot in my tie, a television camera recorded the gesture on a screen in the booking room.

It was six-thirty in the morning but the jail was as loud as if it had been six-thirty at night. The jail was built in the basement of the courthouse, and there were, of course, no windows, only the intense, white fluorescent lights that buzzed overhead. The jail was a place where people waited out their time and yet without day or night time stood still; only mealtimes and the change of guards communicated the passage of time to the inmates.

I moved out of the way of a trustie who raced by carrying trays of food. Breakfast that morning, the last day of July, was oatmeal, canned fruit cocktail, toast, milk and Sanka. Jones stepped into the hall from the kitchen and acknowledged me with an abrupt nod. He had done his hair up in cornrows and his apron was splattered with oatmeal. Jones cooked for the population. He was also a burglar and an informant and his one great fear was coming to trial and being sentenced to time at the state prison in Folsom. Several of his ex-associates were there, thanks to his help. I had just been granted a further continuance of his trial, delaying it for another sixty days. Our strategy was to string out his case as long as possible so that when he inevitably pled guilty he would be credited with the time he served in county jail and avoid Folsom altogether. The district attorney's office was cooperative; the least they owed him was county time — easy time, the prisoners called it. County was relatively uncrowded and the sheriffs relatively benign. On the other hand, county stank like every other jail I'd ever been in. The stink was a complex odor of ammonia, unwashed bodies, latrines, dirty linen and cigarette smoke compounded by bad ventilation and mingled with a sexual musk, a distinctive genital smell. The walls were faded green, grimy and scuffed. The floor, oddly enough, was spotless. The trusties mopped it at all hours of the day and night. Busy work, I suppose.

Everyone in the public defender's office avoided the jail rotation. If the law was a temple, it was built on human misery and jails were the cornerstones. I minded the jail less than most, finding it — psychologically, at least — not so much different from a courtroom. So much of crime and punishment consisted of merely waiting for something to happen, for a case to move. But it was different, the jail, from the plush law school classroom, just a few miles away, from which I graduated ten years earlier determined to do good, to be good. I achieved at least one of those things. I was a good lawyer, and most days that was enough. I was aware, however, that I took refuge in my profession, as unlikely as that seemed considering the amount of human suffering I dealt with. It offered me a role to escape into, from what I no longer knew; perhaps nothing more significant than my own little ration of suffering.

I went into my office, a small room tucked away at the end of a corridor and where it was almost possible to hear yourself think. I picked up a sheaf of papers, arrest reports and booking sheets, the night's haul. There was the usual array of vagrants and drunk drivers, a couple of burglaries, a trespass. One burglary, involving two men, was the most serious of the cases so I gave it special attention. The two suspects were seen breaking into a car in the parking lot of a Mexican restaurant on El Camino. The police recovered a trunkful of car stereos, wires still attached. The suspects were black men in their early twenties with just enough by way of rap sheets to appeal to a judge's hanging instinct. I gathered the papers together and went into the booking office.

"Good morning, Henry," Novack drawled, looking up from the sports page. He had a pale, pudgy face and a wispy little moustache above a mouth set in a perpetual smirk. Novack treated me with the same lazy contempt with which he treated all civilians, not holding the fact that I was a lawyer against me. This made us friends of a sort.

"Good morning, deputy," I replied.

"We had ourselves a little bit of excitement here last night," he said, folding his paper. "Los Altos brought in a drunk — that's what they thought he was, anyway — and it took three of us to subdue him."

"What was he on?"

"Well we took a couple of sherms off of him when we finally got him stripped and housed, so it was probably PCP."

"Why didn't I see an arrest report for him?"

"We couldn't book him until he came down enough to talk. Here's his papers."

I took the papers and asked, "Where's he at now?"

"In the drunk tank with the queens. He's a fag."

"That's no crime," I reminded him.

"Good thing, too, or we'd have to charge admission around here."

I read the report. The suspect's name was Hugh Paris. He stood five-foot ten, had blond hair and blue eyes. He refused to give an address or answer questions about his employment or his family. He had no criminal record. I studied his booking photo. His hair was in his face and his eyes went off in two different directions, but there was no denying he was an exceptionally handsome man.

"How do you know he's gay?" I asked.

"They picked him up outside of that fag bar in Cupertino," Novack said.

"He was arrested for being under the influence of PCP, possession of PCP, resisting arrest and battery on an officer. Geez, did the arresting officer go through the penal code at random?" Novack scowled at me. "Was anyone hurt?"

"Just scuff marks, counsel."

"Was he examined by a doctor to determine whether he was under the influence?"

"Nope."

"Did you ask him to submit to a urine test?"

"Nope."

"Then all you can really prove against him is drug possession."

"Well," Novack said, "I guess that's a matter of interpretation between you and the D.A. Are you going to want to see the guy?"

"I'll talk to him," I replied, "but first I'll want to interview these two," and I read him the names of the burglars.

□

I interviewed the burglary suspects separately. They were bored but cooperative. They knew the system as well as I did. They had nothing by way of defense so the best I could do for them was try to plead them to something less serious than burglary. I'd observed that repeat offenders were the easiest to deal with, treating their lawyers with something akin to professional courtesy. All they wanted was a deal. It was only the first timers who bothered to tell you they were innocent. After the interviews ended, I walked back to the booking office and poured myself a cup of Novack's coffee. I flipped him a quarter and asked to see Hugh Paris.

They brought him in in handcuffs and a pair of jail blues so big that they fell from his shoulders and nearly covered his bare feet. His eyes were focused but he still looked disheveled. I thought, irrelevantly, of a picture of a saint I had seen as a boy, as he was being led off to his martyrdom. There was a glint of purity in Hugh Paris's eyes completely at odds with everything that was happening around him. The guard sat him down in the chair across from mine. I took out a legal pad and set it down on the table between us. I introduced myself as Henry Rios, from the public defender's office.

"A lawyer?" he asked, thickly.

"That's right," I said. "How do you feel, Mr. Paris?"

He gave me a puzzled look as if how he felt should be obvious, and asked, "Are the handcuffs necessary?"

"The sheriffs think so," I said, studying him. "Do you think you'd be all right without them?"

"I'm not going to hurt you."

I had decided he was down from whatever drug he had taken. I called in the deputy and asked him to remove the handcuffs. He resisted but, in the end, the handcuffs went. He stationed himself outside the door. I got up and closed it.

"Better?" I asked.

Paris smiled, revealing a set of even, white teeth. He rubbed his wrists and smoothed his hair, buttoned the top buttons of the jail jumpsuit and pulled himself up in the chair. He looked less dazed now, and he fixed me with a look of appraisal.

"Thank you," he said. "I feel terrible. Why am I here?"

"You were arrested," I replied, and read him the charges.

"Mr. Rios," he said, "I don't remember much about last night, but I do know that I didn't take any drugs."

"None?"

"I smoked a joint and then I went to this bar."

"What's the last thing you remember?"

"I was having a drink," he said, "and then I heard this horrible, rasping noise. It scared the hell out of me. And then I realized it was my own breathing. Then I went outside, I think, because I remember the lights. And then I woke up here. That's it."

"The police found a couple of sherms in your clothes," I said, testing him.

"What's a sherm?" he asked.

"Cigarettes dipped into PCP."

"I don't smoke," he replied, conversationally. It was possible he was telling the truth.

"Were you alone at the bar?"

"I came with an ex-boyfriend," he said, calmly, "but he left before any of this happened."

"You smoke the joint with him?"

"Yes."

"Did you know anyone else at the bar?"

"Not that I remember."

"How many drinks did you have?"

"Two or three. Not more than three."

"What's your friend's name?"

"I don't want him involved."

I had been taking notes. I put down my pen and leaned back into the chair. "There isn't anyone in this room but you and me," I began. "Anything you say to me is privileged. The resisting and battery charges won't stick and they have no evidence you were under the influence of PCP because they didn't bother to have you examined by a doctor. That just leaves the possession charge. If you were just holding it for someone, I might get the charge reduced or even dismissed."

"You don't believe me," he said.

"I have to argue evidence," I said, "and the evidence is, first, you were high on something last night and, second, the police found PCP on you. It shouldn't be hard to see what inference can be drawn from those two facts."

"I know what PCP is," he said, "but I've never used it and I've certainly never carried it on me."

"It could've been in the joint you smoked with your friend," I said. "Let me at least talk to him."

He shook his head. "I have to take care of this my own way."

"You have money to hire your own lawyer?"

"Money isn't the problem," he said, dismissing the thought with a shrug. He looked away from me and seemed to withdraw into himself. I could hear the deputy outside the door shouting at a trustie. Paris looked back at me without expression. The silence went on for a second too long. "You're gay," he said.

Still looking into his eyes, I said, "Yes, I am."

"I didn't think so at first."

"What gave me away?"

"You didn't react at all when I mentioned my boyfriend. You didn't even blink. Straight men always give themselves away."

I shrugged. "There probably isn't anything you could tell me about yourself or your boyfriend that would surprise me. So why not level with me about last night?"

"I have," he said, wearily. "Look, it was Paul's joint and

maybe it was laced with PCP. He could've given me the cigarettes. I just don't remember."

"Then let's call him and clear it up."

"I can't."

"Why?"

"I'm hiding," he said. "I shouldn't have called Paul in the first place. I can't risk seeing him again."

"Who are you hiding from?"

"I'm sorry," he said. "I can't tell you, although I'd like to."

"Then take my card," I said, digging one out from my wallet, "and call me when you want to talk."

He studied the card and said, "Thanks. I'd like to make a phone call."

"I'll take care of that," I said. I reached across the table to shake his hand. This we did very formally. Then the deputy knocked and I called him in to take the prisoner back to his cell.

□

Outside it was a bright and balmy morning. A fresh, warm wind lifted the tops of the palm trees that lined the streets and sunlight glittered on the pavement. I put on my sunglasses and headed toward California Avenue where I was meeting my best friend, Aaron Gold, for breakfast. He had told me he had a business proposition to make. A couple of kids cycled by with day packs strapped to their shoulders. The Southern Pacific commuter, bound for San Francisco, rumbled by at the end of the street. I felt a flash of restlessness as it passed. Another summer passing. In two months I would be thirty-four.

"Henry," I heard Gold call. I looked up from where I'd stopped, in front of a pet store. He approached rapidly, his intelligent, simian face balled into a squint against the sunlight. He was tall, pale, a little thick around the waist, but he still carried himself like the college jock he'd been.

"Morning, Aaron."

"What were you thinking about?" he asked.

"Nothing really. Getting older."

He made a derisive little noise. "You're still a kid. Look at me, I'm pushing forty. Am I worried?"

"You're in your prime," I said, not altogether jokingly. In his tailored suit, Gold looked sleek and prosperous from his polished shoes and manicured nails to the fifty dollar haircut that tamed his curly, black hair.

"You never went to my tailor," he said, looking me over critically. "Come on, let's eat." He took me by the elbow and led me across the street into the restaurant where all the waitresses knew him by name. We found a table at the back, ordered breakfast and drank our first cups of coffee in silence.

Thirteen years earlier, Gold and I had been assigned as roommates in the law school dormitory our first year there. We had not liked each other much at first. He mistook my shyness for arrogance and I failed to see that his arrogance masked his shyness. Things sorted themselves out and we became friends. He was one of the first people I told I was gay. It would be an exaggeration to say he took it well, but we remained friends on the levels that counted most, respect and trust. Lately, he had even relaxed a little about my homosexuality — joking that I needed to meet a nice Jewish boy and settle down.

He was saying, "Did you run into anyone I know at the jail?"

"You don't go to county jail for SEC violations," I replied.

"Trading stock on insider information isn't the only criminal activity my clients engage in."

"Doubtless, but they wouldn't stoop to the services of a public defender."

"Actually," he said, "that brings me to the subject of this meeting, your future."

"It's secure as long as there's crime in the streets."

"There's crime in the boardrooms, too, Henry. My firm is interested in hiring an associate with a criminal law background. I've circulated your name. People are impressed."

"Why would your firm dirty its hands in criminal practice?"

Gold put his coffee cup down and said, "Corporations consist of people, some of whom are remarkably venal. Others still are just plain stupid. Anyway, they've come to us often enough needing a criminal defense lawyer to make it worth our while to hire one. We'd start you as a third-year associate, at sixty thousand a year."

I answered quickly, "Well, thanks for thinking of me, but I'm not interested."

Gold said, "Look, if it's the money, I know you deserve more, but that's just starting pay."

"You know it's not the money, Aaron," I said, reflecting that the sum he named was almost double my present wage.

He sighed and said, "Henry, don't tell me it's the principle." I said nothing. "You're wasting yourself in the public defender's office. You knock yourself out for some little creep and what you get in return is a shoebox of an office and less money than a first-year associate at my firm makes."

"So I should exchange it for a bigger office and more money and the opportunity to defend some rising young executive who gets busted for drunk driving?"

"Why not? Aren't the rich entitled to as decent a defense as the poor?"

"You never hear much public outcry over the quality of legal representation of the rich."

"What is it you want?" he asked, his voice rising. "The rosy warm glow that comes from doing good? You're not dealing with political prisoners, you're dealing with crooks and murderers."

"It's true they don't recruit criminals from country clubs, but if they're outsiders, so am I."

"Because you're gay," he said, flatly, dropping his voice. "If you're gay."

"That's settled."

"I won't argue the point now," he said, "but you let it run your life, closing doors for you. If you really were gay and accepted it, you would make your choices on other grounds than whether someone would object."

"I can think of plenty of reasons for not joining your firm," I replied, "none of them related to being gay."

"They aren't why you'll turn me down," he said.

I laid my fork aside and glanced out the window. It was luminous with summer light. Gold and I had a variation of this conversation nearly every time we talked. Since each of our positions was set in stone, the only thing our talking accomplished was to get us angry at each other.

"Every choice closes doors," I said, "and at some point you are left in the little room of yourself. I think most people who get to that room go crazy because they're surrounded with missed possibilities and no principle to explain or justify why they made the choices they did. I don't invite unhappiness, Aaron. Avoiding conflict may not be the noblest principle, but it works for me."

"Can you say you're happy?"

"No, can you?"

"No, but there are substitutes."

I didn't need to ask him what his substitutes were, I knew. Work was at the top of the list. In fact, work was the whole of his list. It had been mine, too, but recently I'd lost a big case and word had it I was burned out. Maybe I was, but if so, what was my alternative to work? I had never thought to cultivate any. The waitress came around and I offered her my cup for coffee, promising myself I would sit down later and think about the future, hoping it would creep up on me before I had the chance. I told Aaron about my jailhouse interviews.

"Hugh Paris," Gold said, "that name is familiar."

"Think he trades stock on insider information?"

"Maybe he's rich." I shook my head. "You'd be surprised," Gold continued, "at the number of the rich in our little town. They may not control their money, or know exactly where it comes from, but it dribbles in, from trusts, stocks, annuities."

"Whether or not he was rich," I said, "I wish he'd talked to me. He looked like he was carrying a secret he needed badly to unload."

"Another missed possibility?" Gold asked as he reached for the check. I let him take it.

□

It was a little after eight when I got to my office on the fourth floor of the courthouse. There were already people waiting in the reception room, thumbing through the inevitable packets of official looking papers that criminal defendants seem to generate as they go through the system. The receptionist had not yet come in, so they stopped me as I walked through and I tried to answer their questions. Finally, I made it to the door that seperated us from our clients. I walked down the narrow corridor, made narrower by the presence of file cabinets, for which there was no other space, pushed against the walls. I passed my small, sunless office and headed toward the lounge.

Frances Kelly, the supervising attorney, sat at a table with the daily legal journal spread out in front of her. She let a cigarette burn between her fingers, lifting it to her lips just as the ash fell, dropping on the lapel of her jacket.

She looked up at me as I poured myself some coffee. "Did you know Roger Chaney?" she asked.

"Not well," I answered. "He left the office just as I was coming in."

"Excellent lawyer," she said. "He and I trained together, shared an office. He helped me prepare for my first trial."

"Is there something about him in the journal?" I asked, sitting across from her as she lit another cigarette.

"He's being arraigned today in federal court in San Francisco," she said, "on a conspiracy to distribute cocaine charge."

"Roger Chaney?" I asked, incredulously. "I thought you were going to tell me he'd been elevated to the bench."

"With Roger," she replied, "it could've gone either way."

"Are the charges true, then?"

"I know he had a very successful practice defending some big dealers, and he was making a lot of money, but that was never the lure of the law for him."

"No? Then what?"

She rose heavily, an elegant fat woman in a linen suit with black hair and beautiful, clear eyes, and ambled to the coffee urn. "He was an intellectual virtuoso," she said, "convinced he could talk circles around any other lawyer or judge, and he was right. But the courtroom isn't the real world."

"He thought he could get away with something?"

"We must presume him innocent," she said, piously, "but he had that kind of vanity." After a second she added, "So do you."

She headed for the door and motioned for me to follow. We went into her office, the only one with a window. Outside, a thin layer of smog rose in the direction of San Jose, but the view to the brown hills surrounding the university was clear as they rolled beyond the palm trees and red tile roofs.

Frances was saying, "I sometimes think really brilliant people shouldn't be permitted to practice law. They get bored too easily and cause trouble."

"Are you about to pass along some advice?"

She laughed. "I just wanted to know how you are, Henry. You've been with us three months and we haven't had much chance to talk." She referred to my forced transfer from the main office in San Jose to this branch office. The topic of conversation, my mental health, now came into focus as sharply as the yellow rose in the vase at the edge of Frances' desk. I was annoyed by both.

"Considering that my transfer was against my will, I'm fine."

"I had nothing to do with the transfer," she said. "You're not being put out to pasture, just given a rest after your last trial."

"Which I lost," I said. "That was the real reason I got kicked down from felony trials to arraignments."

"The jury convicted him," she said, "and no one faults your work which, considering the circumstances, was excellent." I didn't know whether by circumstances she referred to the fact that only a few I.Q. points separated my client from a vegetable or the fact that he used an axe handle to bludgeon his elderly parents to death. A series of coroner's photographs passed through my mind. Pained by the recollection, I touched my fingers to my forehead. She caught the gesture and tactfully looked away.

"The circumstances were of no interest to the jury," I said. "They sent him to Death Row."

"That's on appeal."

"And I was farmed out here, to rusticate."

"You object to my company?" She expelled a gust of cigarette smoke that passed through the sunlight like a cloud.

"But seriously," I replied.

"To rest," she said, "from the pressures of trial court. I could see the burn-out on your face when you first got here."

"Send me back," I said. "I've done nothing but interview clients for other lawyers and sit in arraignment court haggling with the D.A. over public nuisance cases."

"Whether you go back is not my call."

"Whether?" I demanded. "Not when? Call San Jose and tell them that I didn't crack up, after all. Tell them I'm burned out from the other end. I mean, you all think I'm demoralized or exhausted from my work, but I'm not. It's the rest of my life I'm burned out on. This job keeps me going." I heard the tremor in my voice so I cut myself short.

"I'm not proposing to take your job away," she replied. "Everyone in the office knows you're one of the best lawyers we have." She put out her cigarette in an onyx ashtray and lit another. "The office has just hired a dozen new lawyers, most fresh out of law school. They're looking for someone to train them. The job is yours if you want it."

"That's the second-best offer I've had this morning," I said. She looked puzzled. "It's nothing. I don't see myself as a teacher."

"You have so much to pass along."

"I'm thirty-three, Frances, not sixty-three. I'm not ready to sit on the veranda and tell war stories."

"Think about it," she said. She noticed me looking at the rose and she plucked it from the vase and handed it to me.

"And if I don't take the job, my exile continues."

"The rose is from my garden," she replied.

"My favorite flower," I said, standing.

□

In my office, I dropped the rose into the trash can and sat down. There was a pile of cases to be reviewed before I went down to arraignment court that afternoon. There was also a list of clients to be interviewed and advised, and cases to be assigned to other lawyers. I opened the first file and thought, immediately, of Hugh Paris sitting in his cell downstairs. And here, I told myself, I sit in my cell upstairs. I dismissed the thought as self-pity compounded with a pang of lust. But the little room was too warm, suddenly, and I could not concentrate on the papers before me.

I got up and went into the bathroom where I washed my face in cold water. Looking at the mirror, I studied that face carefully. I pressed my fingers, lightly, at the corners of my eyes, smoothing out the wrinkles and I looked, almost, twenty-five again. I could quit and start over, I told the reflection in the mirror. My eyes answered, start what over? What is there?

Another lawyer came in, and I turned from the mirror, said hello to him and went back to my office.

The morning dragged on as I shuffled files from one side of my desk to the other. Outside my office, I heard the babble of voices as the other lawyers interviewed clients and witnesses or hurried off to court shouting last minute questions about a legal issue or a particular judge's temperment. I felt the excitement but did not share it.

There comes a point in the career of every criminal defense lawyer when he realizes that what keeps him in practice are his prejudices not his principles. Suspicion of authority and contempt for the platitudes with which injustice too often cloaks itself can take you a long way but, ultimately, they are no substitute for the simple faith that what you are doing is right. It came to me, as I sat there buried in papers, that I had lost that faith.

I left a message with Frances's secretary that I wanted to see her after lunch, then went off to a nearby bar and had a couple of drinks. As I sat on the barstool cracking peanuts and sipping my bourbon, my thoughts veered back to Hugh Paris.

It was nothing as trivial as lust. Seeing him had precipitated this crisis because I had not been able to help him, though I wanted to. And, after all, what did my help amount to? Getting someone less time in jail than otherwise or even getting him off were often temporary respites in long-term downward slides. That was the extent of the assistance I could offer — dispensing placebos to the terminally ill.

Frances was in her office when I knocked at the door. She beckoned me in and I sat down, swallowing the mint I'd been chewing to mask the bourbon on my breath. It was important that she not know I had been drinking.

"Frances, I've made a decision."

"You'll teach the class?"

"No." I gripped my hands together in my lap. "I'm quitting."

"What?" She stared at me.

"I called San Jose and told them. I wanted to tell you, too. I wanted to thank you for your many kindnesses—" I stopped. The air between us buzzed with inarticulate feeling.

"Henry, you can't mean this. Take a few days off, a few weeks if you want. Travel."

I shook my head. "I hate traveling. I have no hobbies. I'm thirty-three years old and all I know about life is what I learned in law school or the inside of a courtroom. And it's pathetically little, Frances." She reached for a cigarette. "I know I'm a little old for it, but I believe I'm having an identity crisis."

"That's no reason to quit your job," she replied.

"This is more than my job, it's my life. And it's not enough." I rose. "Do you understand?"

"No. Do you?"

"Not very clearly." I sat down again. "I met a man in the jail this morning, an inmate. I wanted to help him, to offer him some kind of comfort, something human. But all I knew how to do was deliver speeches."

"We offer people what no one else can give them," Frances said, "a possible way out of their trouble. Is that so insignificant?"

"Of course not, when it works. But so often it doesn't, and anyway," I laid my hands on her desk, "what does that give me?"

She sighed. "Well that's the key, isn't it? If you've reached the point of asking that question then whatever you're getting from it is obviously not enough."

"Wish me luck."

"No," she said. "I'll wish you'll change your mind."

"I won't."

"All right," she said, "then good luck."

I went back to my office and cleaned out my desk. Some of the other lawyers drifted in, stood around nervously, said a few well-intended words. By three o'clock I'd done nearly everything I needed to do to extricate myself from my job. Just before I left I called down to the jail. Hugh Paris had been bailed out by someone who signed the bail receipt as John Smith. I gathered up the last of my papers and left.

– 2 –

I was awake the second I heard the movement in the shrubs outside the bedroom window. I glanced at the clock on the bedstand; it was a little after three a.m. The soft but distinctive shuffle of footsteps echoed outside and then I heard a quick rap at the front door. I got out of bed, pulled on a pair of pants and went into the living room. I stood near the door and listened. The last time I had been awakened at that hour was by a disgruntled, drunken client who wanted to break my legs. He might have, too, had he not passed out while we were talking.

There was another knock, louder and more urgent. I peered through the peephole. Hugh Paris stood shivering in the dark. He wore a pair of jeans and a gray polo shirt. I was startled to see him but not surprised. In the two weeks since I'd seen him at the jail, I'd thought of him often, the way one thinks of unfinished business. The thought of him nagged at the back of my mind for a lot of reasons, not the least of which was his beautiful, calm face. One could ascribe any kind of character, from priest to libertine, to his remote and handsome face. A breeze blew his hair across his forehead. He touched his knuckles to the door and rapped harder. I opened it enough for him to see me.

"Don't turn on any lights," he said. "I think I was followed."

"Come in." I opened the door a little wider and he slipped through. I ordered him to stand still and patted him down for weapons. He wasn't even carrying a wallet. "All right," I said. "Come over to my desk. I have a reading lamp that will give us enough light without attracting attention." He followed me and sat down. I touched the light switch and his face leapt forward from the darkness like a flame.

He said, "I could use a drink."

"First tell me how you got my address."

"I called your office yesterday, and when they told me you quit I convinced the receptionist that we'd gone to college together and I was passing through town and wanted to surprise you." He shivered I went over to the kitchen counter and brought back a bottle of Jack Daniels and two glasses. As he drank, I noticed for the first time that he was about my age — not younger, as I'd remembered. The skin beneath his eyes was pouched with fatigue, as though he had awakened from a long sleep. He set his empty glass on the desk, and I moved the bottle toward him. The liquor brought the color back to his face.

"When someone comes to visit me at this hour, I assume it's not just to chat," I said.

"I need a place to stay tonight."

"And you don't have any better friends?" He poured himself another drink. I caught the glint of his watch. It was very thin and elegant, mounted on a black leather strap. I had seen watches like that before. They went along with trust funds, prep schools and names ending with Roman numerals.

Hugh was saying something. I asked, "What?"

"You asked me if I had any better friends and I said no. I came down from the city."

"And you were followed? By whom?"

"It's a long story," he said, and, as if as an afterthought he added, "I only need the bed for the night." His inflection was sexual and I thought about it for a second before responding.

"As flattering as it is, I can't believe you came here to proposition me," I said, "which is not to say that couldn't be part of the deal. But why don't you tell me what you really want."

He smiled, charmingly, ruefully. "All right, Henry. I may not look like it but I come from money. Old and famous money. A lot of it has been spent to keep me out of San Francisco."

"Why?"

"My grandfather controls the money, and he hates me."

"Because you're gay?"

"That probably has something to do with it," he said, lightly. "There have been other problems through the years."

"Drugs?" I guessed, remembering the circumstances of his arrest.

"You've seen hypes before?" I nodded. He held his right arm out beneath the dim yellow light. I saw bluish bruises clustered at intervals up and down his vein. They were faint and there were no recent marks or scabs.

"You stopped using?"

"Six months ago. I told my grandfather. He was not impressed."

"Who is he?"

"Robert Paris," he said, as if each syllable was significant.

I thought for a second the name meant something to me but recognition faded as quickly as it came.

"The name is not familiar."

"No? It doesn't mean anything to most people but I thought you might recognize it." I shook my head and he shrugged. "I think he had me followed tonight."

"Why? If he hates you, why should he concern himself with your whereabouts?"

"Money. I have certain rights to the family fortune," he said, lifting his glass. "My grandfather would like to extinguish them."

"You mean with some legal action?"

"No," he replied, softly, "I mean murder." He drained his glass. I knew at once that he believed what he was saying, but I did not believe it. From my experience, I did not believe in premeditated murder any more than an agnostic believes in God and for the same reason; there never was any proof. Whether a killing occurs in an instant or years after some remembered slight, no killer is ever in his right mind when he kills. For me, that ruled out premeditation.

"You're exaggerating," I said.

"No. He's killed before." He smiled, bleakly. "I'm not making this up. You don't know my grandfather."

"Rich people don't go around planning to kill each other. They use lawyers, instead."

Hugh laughed and said, "Not someone who thinks he's above the law. Henry, I don't mean he's going to kill me himself or hire someone to shoot me in broad daylight. I'm sure it would be arranged to look like an accident or a suicide."

I shook my head. "That's unbelievable. I've known murderers. I've represented them and one or two I even got off. The perfect passionless murder does not exist. Killing is a sloppy business."

"Have any of your murderers been rich?" I told him no. He continued, "I didn't think so. Money buys a lot of insulation and silence. My grandfather could have us both killed and no one would ever suspect him." He poured himself another drink and said, "I see by your face you don't believe me."

"I believe that you think you're in danger. I'm not sure what you want from me."

"You heard me out," he said. "That's all I wanted. And a bed. Wasn't that the deal?"

"I guess so," I said, aware, suddenly, of the nearness of his body and the noise of his breathing and the darkness of the room around us. We rose, wordlessly, and went into the bedroom.

□

I woke up alone and lay back, watching the shadow of the tree outside the window sway across the wall. The only noises were the clock ticking and the wind. The sheets and blankets were kicked back and over the foot of the bed. A wadded up towel lay crumpled on the floor among Hugh's scattered clothes. The detritus of passion. I sat myself up against the wall and studied my nakedness impassively. I kept myself in shape out of habit and thought about my body only when it was sick, hurt, or hungry.

Once as an adolescent and twice as an adult, I had been in love, the last time having been four years earlier. Except for those times, sex was largely a matter of one-night stands. It wasn't the best arrangement, but, I told myself, it was all that I had time for. Now that my career had come to an abrupt halt, there was a lot of time, more time than I'd ever had as an adult. Enough time to go crazy, or fall in love again. I got out of bed and dressed.

Stepping into the living room I saw him, wearing an old blue robe of mine, pacing the patio. From where I stood, he looked like a figure projected on a screen, luminous, distant and larger than life. He seemed to me at that moment the sum of every missed opportunity in my life. I let the feeling pass. He saw me, smiled, drew open the door and came into the room.

"You're finally awake."

"Yes, I like watching you. Hungry?"

"No, but how about some coffee?" I told him I would brew a pot. "I guess I should get dressed." He disappeared into the bedroom emerging a few minutes later pulling on his shirt.

I handed him a mug of coffee and said, "Let's go back outside." We stepped out on the patio to a brilliant day. The smells of the potted plants hung in the air, musky and carnal. "What are you going to do?"

"Go back to the city."

"And your grandfather?"

"He'll find me when he wants to." He sipped his coffee. "And you?"

"I've decided to set up my own practice and there's a lot to be done to get ready."

He nodded as if I'd said something significant. The air between us was thick with unspoken words. I reached over and touched his arm briefly. He smiled.

"Did you always want to be a lawyer?"

"No, I drifted into it from graduate school. I wanted to change the world and law offered more opportunities than history."

"Did you know you were gay when you started law school?"

"I've always known."

"It doesn't seem to be a problem with you."

"Is it with you?"

"No one ever prepared me for it," he said, "or the experience of feeling different even though you don't appear different to other people."

I nodded. The sexual aspect of homosexuality was, in many ways, the least of it. The tough part was being truthful without painting yourself into a corner: I am different, but not as different as you think.

Aloud, I said, "It's schizophrenic, isn't it?" At once Hugh's face changed. The placid blond handsomeness dissolved and was replaced by anger.

"Don't use that word around me. You don't have any idea of what schizophrenia is like."

"I just meant—"

"That it's an identity crisis? It's the end of identity. It's death."

Startled by his outburst, I mumbled an apology. The fierceness went out of his eyes but not the distance. The intimacy between us was shattered and I could not think of any words to call him back.

"I'm all right, just sort of keyed up, I guess. I should be going now."

"I'm really sorry, Hugh," I said, again.

"You couldn't've known," he said, more to himself than me. "I'd like to see you again. I'll call."

"Sure. I'd like that." We stood facing each other, but it seemed absurd to shake hands, so we just smiled, like two strangers who had collided by accident.

□

A week after Hugh's nocturnal visit, I met Aaron Gold for drinks at a bar on University Avenue called Barney's to talk about my future, again. Gold had been in solo practice in San Francisco for a couple of years before joining his current firm, and I relied on him for advice on setting up on my own. His years as an associate with a rich, prestigious firm had not eradicated his memories of the privations of his first practice.

Gold liked advising me. It allowed him to relive his days on his own when he expected to build a powerful firm from his own ambition and drive. In the end, he decided the world was insufficiently impressed and he signed on with a firm in town. A good firm, the best in the area and successful enough to have branch offices, but, after all, not a New York firm or even one in San Francisco.

His choice puzzled me. As an editor of law review, Gold could have written his ticket anywhere in the country, but he stayed in our backwater university town far from the centers of the power and influence he'd once set out to dazzle. And he had become a real company man, absolutely dedicated to the firm and annoyingly secretive about his work.

We were getting along pretty well, Gold and I, I thought as I stepped into the bar from the muggy August afternoon. However, some aspects of my life remained a problem for him as I discovered again when I brought up the subject of Hugh Paris.

"You went to bed with a client?" he asked incredulously as the startled cocktail waitress brought our drinks.

"He's not a client," I said after she'd gone. "I didn't take his case."

"It's the appearance of impropriety you should be concerned about."

"Look, I haven't exactly advertised the news. I was just telling you."

He set his drink down and asked, "Why?"

"You asked what was new with me. I told you."

"Some things you can omit."

"Listen, Aaron, I get to thrill to your accounts of your latest girlfriend, but you treat me like a eunuch. You confide in me, but I can't confide in you? Are we friends, or what?"

He rubbed his forehead and sighed, dramatically. "Yes, we're friends. It's just that — well, in addition to the fact that you're gay — this Paris guy sounds like trouble. You should marry or something."

"Hugh's all right," I said, defensively, and added, "and as for marriage, you're nearly six years older than me and not married."

"That's different. I got into law late and I have to make up for lost time if I want to make partner before I'm forty. Then I'll marry. A man can marry at any time."

"If it makes you that uncomfortable for me to talk about being gay, I'll stop talking about it."

He waved his hand as though waving away a fly. "It's part of your life. It's just difficult. Give me time."

"I told you ten years ago."

"What, in law school? Everyone was something in law school. Marxists, feminists, homosexuals — I was a socialist. It was all theory, then. It didn't mean anything. I never thought you were serious. Let's have another drink." He summoned the waitress.

"Did we sell out?"

"Sell out what?" He lifted an eyebrow. "What did we have to sell? Nothing. We had nothing. It's now that we all have something to sell, and to lose." He raised his glass and touched it against mine in an ironic toast.

□

For the next two days, I reviewed my options. Setting up practice in San Francisco was out of the question because of the expense and the fact that there were too many criminal defense lawyers there already, scrambling for a living. When I'd been transferred out of the Public Defender's office in San Jose, I had burned too many bridges to find my way back. So, for the time being, I decided to stay where I was.

I rented a suite in an office building within walking distance of the courthouse. I bought a desk, installed a phone, and had a nameplate nailed to the door. My business cards were in the process of being printed. All I needed were clients. Since my practice had centered in San Jose, I had very little local reputation and knew I would have to rely, initially, on appointments to criminal cases from which the public defenders disqualified themselves. I had already decided that I did not want a civil law practice.

Appointments represented a steady source of income. Lawyers were appointed from a list maintained by the judges; one applied to be placed on the list. Appointments were sought after and placement on the lists was dictated by political considerations, which, in the world of a small town, meant appeasing those in a position to make life difficult for you. For the judges that meant the D.A. and the public defenders who not only belonged to the same union, but, between them, handled virtually all the criminal matters. The judges were unlikely to appoint any lawyer who had antagonized one or the other office. Therefore, I found it necessary to go make my peace with my ex-employer. I had set up an appointment to see Frances Kelly, to ask her pardon and to get her as a reference.

I climbed the five flights of stairs to the public defender's office in the courthouse. By the time I got there I was sweaty from exertion and nervousness. The reception room was almost empty as I stepped up to the counter and gave my name. The receptionist was new. It had been a little less than a month since I'd quit but it seemed like a year, chiefly because nothing had changed. Even the calendar on the wall was still turned to July. A couple of my ex-colleagues passed through on their way to court. They saw me but said nothing. Omerta, I thought — apparently, I had become a nonperson.

Fifteen minutes later, Frances's secretary appeared and led me to her office, never once acknowledging that she knew me. I wondered if I would get the same reception from Frances. I knocked at her door and entered on her command.

She greeted me with friendly curiousity, rising slightly from behind her desk, extending a braceleted hand. "You look well," she said.

"Thanks. So do you." And, in fact, she looked as sleek and opulent as ever, carrying her avoirdupois like a summer parasol. We exchanged civilities and a little office gossip and then, mentally clearing my throat, I shifted subjects. "I have a favor to ask." She smiled. "But first I want to apologize for the abruptness of my departure."

"You're forgiven," she said.

"I'm going to open my own practice."

"Congratulations," she murmured.

"I don't have any clients yet. I plan to apply to the appointments' list."

"That's wise." I grimaced, mentally. This was like pulling teeth.

"I know the politics of the courthouse," I said. "The presiding judge will know my name immediately, probably remember hearing that I quit, and call you for your opinion."

"And you want to know what I'll tell him."

"No," I said. "I'd like you to recommend me."

She smiled. "I see. Well, your old spirit seems to be returning." She lit a cigarette. "Do you need the money?"

"What?"

"Do you need the money, or do you just want to go back to work?"

"It's not the money," I said. I knew I could live for a year on my savings. "I want the work. I'm good at it."

"Yes, of course, but I'm confused. A month ago you left the office saying you needed time to think over your life."

"I've thought about it."

"And all that led to is concluding that you want to go back to doing the same thing you just left? Has anything really changed?" The question was rhetorical. She went on, "I would tell the presiding judge that you're a brilliant lawyer but a troubled man. I would tell him that if I was a defendant I would gladly entrust you with my case but if I was a judge I would be concerned about saddling a client with a potentially sick lawyer."

"Those are hard words, Frances," I said.

"You could try a case with no preparation and do a better job than another lawyer with unlimited time to prepare, but that's not the point. Frankly, I think you would be tempted to wing it because your heart's not in it anymore."

"You're wrong," I said. "I have never walked into a courtroom unprepared."

She pointed to a stack of files sitting on top of a bookcase. "Your last cases," she said. "Nothing had been done on them."

"I carried them in my head."

"That's the problem, Henry. You're carrying too much in your head."

I stood up. "I can't change your mind?"

"Take all the time you need," she said, "and then come back to me. Not only would I recommend you to the list, I'd help you come back to the office if you wanted."

"How am I supposed to know how much time is enough?"

"You'll know," she said, as though making a promise to a child.

□

I sat at my desk watching the sun set from my new office. The air was dense with a buttery light; the golden hour we used to call it at school. I could see the ubiquitous red tile roofs of the university. The undergrads would not be arriving for another month, but the law school would start up again in a week or two. When I had graduated from there, ten years earlier, it seemed my life was a settled thing. I would rise in the public defender's office, do important political work, and there would be a judgeship at the end, perhaps. I started out with all the right credentials, but somewhere along the line the ambiguities of my profession bogged me down. Truth and falsehood, guilt and innocence, law and equity — this was the stuff of my daily bread. Just as I came to see that there were few clear answers in the law, I also saw there were even fewer such answers in my life.

Frances was right. I wasn't ready to step back into the swamp. I wasn't, but I couldn't think of anything else to do with my life. I opened the side drawer and pulled out a bottle of bourbon and a glass. I kept the sunset company a little longer.

□

It was late when I stumbled in and the red light on my phone machine blinked a welcome. I navigated my way to it and played the messages. There were two of them, both from Hugh, a couple of hours apart. The first was brief, tentative, a greeting. The second asked me to meet him in the city the next day, at a bar in the Castro. I erased the messages, took off my shoes, stretched out on the couch and fell into a sodden sleep.

When I awoke it was light out but the room was shadowy. I inhaled the fumes of last night's liquor and sat myself up. My body ached and my head felt as if someone was tightening a wire around my temples. I got myself into the bathroom and swallowed some aspirin. I went into the bedroom and changed into my running clothes. Outside, I forced myself to stretch and set off toward the university.

The first mile was torture. I passed beneath the massive stone arch at the entrance to the school, pulled off the road and threw up. I felt better and ran down the long palm-lined drive to the Old Quad. Lost somewhere in the thicket to my left was the mausoleum containing the remains of the family by whom the university had been founded. Directly ahead of me loomed a cluster of stone buildings, the Old Quad.

I stumbled up the steps and beneath an archway into a dusty courtyard which, with its clumps of spindly bushes and cacti, resembled the garden of a desert monastery. All around me the turrets and dingy stone walls radiated an ominous silence, as if behind each window there stood a soldier with a musket waiting to repel any invader. I looked up at the glittering facade of the chapel across which there was a mosaic depicting a blond Jesus and four angels representing Hope, Faith, Charity, and, for architectural rather than scriptural symmetry, Love. In its gloomy magnificence, the Old Quad never failed to remind me of the presidential palace of a banana republic.

Passing out of the quad I cut in front of the engineering school and headed for a back road that led up to the foothills. There was a radar installation at the summit of one of the hills called by the students the Dish. It sat among herds of cattle and the ruins of stables. It, too, was a ruin, shut down for many years, but when the wind whistled through it, the radar produced a strange trilling that could well be music from another planet.

The radar was silent as I slowed to a stop at the top of the Dish and caught my breath from the upward climb. I was soaked with sweat, and my headache was gone, replaced by giddy disorientation. It was a clear, hot morning. Looking north and west I saw the white buildings, bridges and spires of the city of San Francisco beneath a crayoned blue sky.

The city from this aspect appeared guileless and serene. Yet, when I walked in its streets what I noticed most was how the light seldom fell directly, but from angles, darkening the corners of things. You would look up at the eaves of a house expecting to see a gargoyle rather than the intricate but innocent woodwork. The city had this shadowy presence as if it was a living thing with secrets and memories. Its temperament was too much like my own for me to feel safe or comfortable there.

I looked briefly to the south where San Jose sprawled beneath a polluted sky, ugly and raw but without secrets or deceit. Then I stretched and began the slow descent back into town.

When I got to San Francisco that afternoon, it was one of those days that arrives at the end of summer just as the last tourists are leaving complaining about the cold and fog. The sky was cloudless. I parked my car on 19th and headed down into the Castro.

The sidewalks were jammed and the crowds drifted slowly past bars from which disco music blared and where men sat on barstools looking out the windows. The air smelled of beer and sweat and amyl nitrate. At bus benches and on strips of grass in front of buildings, men sat, stripped of their shirts, sunbathing and watching the flow of pedestrians through mirrored sunglasses. Approaching the bar where I was meeting Hugh, I smelled marijuana, turned my head and saw a couple of kids sharing a joint as they manned a voter registration table for one of the gay political clubs. I stepped into the bar expecting to find more of the carnival but it was nearly empty. The solitary bartender wiped the counter pensively.

I ordered a gin-and-tonic and took it to a table at the back of the room. Plants hung from the ceiling in big ceramic pots and the lighting was so dim that the atmosphere was nocturnal. Here and there in the darkness I saw a glint of polished brass or a mirror. Suspended from the center of the room was a large fan turning almost imperceptibly in the stale air. It was a place for boozy meditation — emotion recollected in alcohol, as someone once told me in another bar — and I was in a contemplative mood. For the first time in my adult life, I could not see any farther into the future than the door through which Hugh now entered.

I watched him step from the brightly-lit doorway into the dimness of the room, weaving slowly between tables as he approached me. He came up to the table, mumbled a greeting and sat down. He'd had some sun since I'd seen him last. His skin was now the color of dried roses, and his hair was a lighter blond than before but just as disheveled. I restrained an impulse to touch him. He leaned back into his chair, into the shadows. The bartender drifted over and stood in front of us a moment before taking Hugh's order. Hugh looked up, ordered mineral water, and turned away, missing the bartender's bright, yearning smile.

"I didn't actually think you'd come," he said in a low, slow voice.

"You could've called sooner. It's been a couple of weeks."

"Too risky," he said, vaguely, as the bartender set a bottle of Perrier before him. "I have to limit my contacts with outside people."

"Still in hiding?"

"You still don't believe me?"

"I don't think anyone's trying to kill you. Something else has got you scared."

"Junkies are fearless," he replied. He reached out to pour from his bottle into his glass, but his hand shook so violently that he spilled the water on the table. He very slowly set the bottle down. Then, swiftly, everything fell into place for me.

I reached across the table and pulled him forward into the light. He did not resist. His skin was feverish to the touch. His pupils were tightly balled up and too bright. I laid his right arm on the table and spotted the mark almost immediately, a reddish pinprick directly above the vein a few inches above his wrist.

"When did you shoot up?"

"Not long ago," he said, licking his lips.

"You told me you were clean."

"I was. I ran into a friend."

"When?"

"I don't remember. Last week? After I saw you."

"Why didn't you call me?"

"I thought I could handle it. I can't. I need help." The princely face was covered with a film of sweat and its muscles sagged as though they were being pulled downward.

"I didn't come here to babysit a hype," I said, standing.

He reached out and grabbed my arm. He opened his mouth but nothing came out. I saw slow motion panic spread across his face. I stood above him for what seemed like a long time. Then, slowly, I eased back down into the chair beside him.

— 3 —

Outside it was dusk. I turned from the window back to the room, fumbling for a light switch. I pushed a button and three lights flickered on, unsteadily, from a brass fixture in the center of the room. Hugh was asleep in the bedroom at the end of the long, narrow entrance corridor. The toilet gurgled from the bathroom where I'd poured out his vomit and flushed it away.

From my law practice I knew that a heroin addict could stay clean long enough to clear his body of the addiction. If he began to use again it took him awhile to become readdicted. Some addicts used casually — chipping, they called it — but sooner or later their habit caught up with them. Hugh was in the first stage of readdiction. His body, recognizing the opiate for what it was — poison — struggled to reject it, making him sick. If he continued using, the sickness would stop and the body would make its lethal adjustments. That he was sick was encouraging because it meant there was still time to prevent his readdiction.

Not that I knew how to prevent it. I poured myself a drink from the bottle of brandy I'd found in the kitchen. When a hype came to me, it wasn't for medical advice or psychological counseling, but simply to stay out of jail. If I did that much for one of them, got him into a hospital or a drug program, then I considered myself successful. As to why someone became addicted or how he rid himself of the habit, those things remained mysteries to me. The only thing I was pretty sure about was that when dealing with an addict, the fact of addiction was more important than the drug. Thinking about Hugh I wished, for his sake, that I knew more.

I wandered aimlessly across the big, bare room. The house had the dank, decaying smell of so many Victorian houses, as if the walls were stuffed with wet newspaper. Hugh's house, only a couple of blocks from Castro, was in a neighborhood undergoing renovation; many of the neighboring houses looked freshly painted or were in the process of reconstruction or were for sale. His house was untouched by this activity. Strips of paint peeled from the banister of the stairs leading up to the porch. Inside, the rooms were painted white, badly, in some spots barely covering the last application of gaudy wallpaper. The wooden floors were scarred and dirty. From the kitchen, the refrigerator shrieked and buzzed, then subsided to a low whine. It wasn't the house of an heir.

Yet there were incongruous, aristocratic touches. There were dazzlingly white sheets on his bed and freshly laundered towels piled in the bathroom. The few pieces of furniture scattered around the house were of obvious quality. The brandy I was drinking was Courvoisier VSOP, and the glass from which I drank it appeared to be crystal.

I found myself at the bookshelves which held a couple of dozen books. Many of them were worn-out paperbacks, Tolkien, Herman Hesse, a volume of Ginsberg — the library of a college sophomore of the sixties. I opened the Ginsberg. Written on the flyleaf were Hugh's name, the year 1971, and the words New Haven. Inspecting the second shelf, I saw the books were poetry, mostly, and by people I'd never heard of. The spine of one volume was cracked and when I opened it a sheaf of pages fell out, fluttering to the floor. I knelt down to pick them up and saw, on the bottom shelf, a framed photograph laid face down. I picked it up with the pages, put the book back together and turned the picture over.

It was the portrait of a woman, a lady, I thought. She may have been as young as fifty. It was hard to tell from the black and white photo whether her hair was white or an ashy shade of blond. Light and darkness had been tactfully deployed on the plain background behind her. The obvious effect was timelessness and the apparent reason was the woman's age. Still, there was an elegance in her angular, handsome face quite apart from the photographer's craft, and a kind of luster in the brightness of her hair and eyes. I thought she must have once been beautiful.

"My mother," a voice commented behind me. I nearly dropped the picture in surprise and turned to find Hugh standing at the edge of the room, just outside the light. He stepped forward, white-faced, his eyes exhausted. "Sorry. I didn't mean to come up on you like that." He held out his hand for the photo and I gave it to him. He studied it a moment then returned it. I laid it back on the bookshelf.

"Nice picture," I said. "Looks professional."

"The official portrait," he said, with a trace of contempt in his voice. "It appears on all the dustjackets."

"She writes?"

He nodded, seating himself on a corner of the couch, drawing a thick sweater across his bare chest. I noticed for the first time, watching him, that the room was cold. "What has she written?"

"Poetry, mostly."

"I didn't notice any of her books on your shelves."

"I don't have any."

"You're not close to her?"

"I haven't seen her in years."

"Does she live in San Francisco?"

"No, in the east. Boston, I think."

"With your father?"

He hesitated a second before saying, "He's dead."

I heard his hesitation with a lawyer's ear and something about it was not quite right, so I asked, "Are you sure?"

"Don't cross-examine me." He shivered and reached to the table for the brandy, swigging it directly from the bottle. Then he put it down and ran a hand through his already disheveled hair. He looked fragile and unhappy.

"I'll make you some coffee," I said, still standing by the books, "if you'll tell me where it is."

"Blue canister in the refrigerator," he said, shivering again.

When I returned to the living room he was standing at the window, which was now black with night, facing himself — a ghostly reflection. I set the mugs of coffee down and went over.

"Something out there?"

"A car passed by, slowly, without its lights on."

"Has that happened before?"

"No," he said, "and maybe it wasn't meant for me." I made a noise in the back of my throat. "You still don't believe that I'm in danger of being killed."

"You're doing a pretty effective job of killing yourself." He turned away, abruptly, went to the table and picked up a cup of coffee.

"I'm sorry about today."

"Do you want to talk about it?"

"I was bored and lonely."

"Some would call that the human condition."

He laughed mirthlessly. "My coping mechanism is easily overwhelmed."

"That sounds like a diagnosis."

"My last analyst," he replied, carelessly, "who also told me that intimacy is difficult for me."

"I hadn't noticed."

"Sex is not the same thing."

"I see. Thank you for setting me straight."

"Wait," he said. "Let's start over. I asked you to come up because I wanted to see you again, not to score points against you."

"All right," I said, crossing over to the couch and sitting down beside him. I lay my hand, tentatively, on his. "Tell me what happened between last weekend and today."

He looked at me intently through cloudy blue eyes, then said, "Have you ever heard of a poet named Cavafy?" I told him no. "A Greek poet. Gay, in fact. He wrote a poem about a young dissolute man who tires of his life and resolves to move to a new city and mend his ways. The poet's comment is that moving away is futile because, having ruined his life in one place, he has ruined it everywhere."

"And?"

"I had so many good reasons for leaving New York and coming home, but when I got here they — evaporated. I was the same person, it was the same life."

"People overcome addictions."

"But not self-contempt." He poured brandy into his coffee cup and leaned back as if to tell a bedtime story. "My grandfather, who raised me after my father died, had very primitive and set notions about what a man is. He never missed an opportunity to let me know that I didn't measure up."

"Let it go," I said, thinking back to my own father. "You'll live to bury him. That changes everything."

"He poisoned my childhood," Hugh said, ignoring me, "and I looked for causes, not knowing they didn't exist, believing that I deserved his abuse."

Something in his tone made me ask, "What kind of abuse, Hugh?"

"He said I was too pretty to be a boy," Hugh replied, his eyes bright with defiance and shame. Slowly, I understood.

"He assaulted you — sexually?"

"The joke is that I already knew I was gay. Knew I was different, anyway. What took me years to learn is that it didn't have—" he paused, searching for words — "to be so demeaning."

"What did he tell you?"

"That I led him on, that I wanted it." He smiled, bitterly. "I was the seductive twelve year old. A few weeks after it happened he sent me to a prep school in the east. Eighteen years ago. I can count on my fingers the times I've seen him since."

"Why have you come back?"

"I'm living on my anger, Henry. It's the only life I've got left in me, and I've come back to confront him. But I need to be strong when I see him, and I'm not strong yet."

"In the meantime, you brood and destroy yourself."

"I thought, in the meantime, you and I could become friends." I heard the ghost of seduction in his voice, yet it was not meant seductively. It was a plea for help. "If only I had met you — even five years ago."

"What's wrong with now?" I asked and drew him close.

□

The next morning I woke to find Hugh standing perfectly still in a wide sunny space near the window, facing the wall above my head, wearing only a pair of faded red sweatpants. He held his hands at his side, fingers splayed, but not stiffly. He breathed, slowly, deeply. His breath filled his entire torso with quivery tension as he inhaled, bringing his chest and abdominal muscles into sharp relief. As he exhaled, his chest fell with delicate control. The color of his skin darkened as the blood rushed in a torrent beneath the skin. Each muscle of his body was elegantly delineated, like an ancient statue that time had rendered human.

He lifted his chin a little, drew his shoulders even straighter and parted his legs, one forward and one back. I watched as he sank to the floor, raising his arms at his side until he was fully extended in a split. There was the slightest tremor in his fingertips giving away the effort but no other part of his body moved. He pulled his back straighter, closed his eyes and held the position until the tremor in his fingers died. Then, he carefully brought his back leg forward in a wide arc, lowering his arms at the same time, until he was sitting. He opened his eyes.

"That was amazing," I said.

"I was so much better once," he replied, shaking his head vigorously, scattering drops of sweat from his hair. "I studied dance in college."

"Where?"

"Where?" he repeated, smiling. "I was at Yale for a couple of years, and N.Y.U. for a semester or two and Vanderbilt for a few months. I moved around."

"Without ever graduating?"

"I never did, no." He stood up, crossed over to the bed, a mattress laid against a corner, and extended his hand. "Get up and I'll take you to breakfast."

I let him pull me out of bed and our bodies tangled. He was flushed and a little sweaty and his hair brushed against the side of my face like a warm wind as we drew each other close.

An hour later we were sitting at a table in a dark, smoky corner of a coffeehouse on Castro. The waiter cleared our breakfast plates and poured more coffee.

"So you still consider yourself a hype?" I asked, pursuing our conversation.

"Of course. I'm addicted whether I use or not because being high is normal for me and how I function best. When I'm not using, I'm anxious."

"I'm pretty anxious myself, sometimes, but I've never felt the desire to obliterate myself."

"It's not just the sedative effect a hype craves. It's also the rush, and the rush is so intense, like coming without sex."

"I've heard that before from my clients. One of them said it was like a little death."

Hugh looked at me curiously and asked, "Do you know what that means?"

"I imagine he meant you lose yourself."

"Exactly. La petite mort — that's what the French called orgasm. They believed that semen is sort of concentrated blood so that each time a man came he shortened his life a little by spilling blood that couldn't be replenished."

"And women?"

"Then, as now, men didn't much concern themselves with how women felt." He finished his coffee. "Let's go for a walk."

Walking down Castro toward Market, Hugh reached over and took my hand. Self-consciously, I left it there. It perplexed me how sex with other men seemed natural to me but not the small physical gestures of affection and concern. What I remembered most clearly from my first sex with another man was the unexpected tenderness. It disturbed me — disoriented me, I guess. I had expected homosexuality to be dark and furtive, but it wasn't. It was shattering but liberating to come out and it ended a lot of doubts that had been eroding my self-confidence. I remember thinking, back then, so this is it, one of the worst things I can imagine happening has happened. And life goes on.

As we rounded the corner of Castro and crossed over to Market, he gently let go of my hand. We were out of the ghetto. I reached over and put my hand back into his. He looked over at me, startled, then tightened his grip. And life went on.

□

There were three messages from Aaron Gold on my answering machine when I got to my apartment, each a little more frantic than the last. I couldn't blame him. I had gone to San Francisco for a day and stayed a week. Finally, tired of wearing Hugh's clothes and needing a little time away from the intensity of our developing relationship, I drove home to pick up the mail and for a change of clothes.

I called Gold's office. His first words were, "Are you all right? I was ready to start calling the hospitals."

"I'm fine. Why are you so alarmed?"

"We were supposed to have dinner on Monday night. It is now Friday."

"Jesus, Aaron. I completely forgot. I should've called from the city."

"The city? Is that where you've been?"

"Yes, at Hugh Paris's."

"He lives there? Where?"

"Why?" There was a long silence on the other end of the line. "Aaron, are you still there?"

"Are you going back up?"

"Tonight," I said.

"I need to see you before you go," he said in a strange voice.

"Sure. When?"

"I'll meet you in an hour at Barney's," he said.

He was already at the bar when I got there, staring, a bit morosely over a tall drink with a lot of fruit jammed into the glass.

"You look like you've lost your best friend," I said, sitting down. Touching his glass, I said, "What's that you're drinking? A Pink Lady?" He said nothing. I added, to provoke him, "Jews really don't have the hang of ordering alcohol."

"You're pretty chipper," he said, sourly. The waitress came over and I ordered a Mexican beer.

"I'm happy, Aaron."

"Hugh Paris?" he asked, with almost a sneer in his voice. "Tell me, what do you really know about him?"

"I'm not sure I understand what you mean."

He waited until I had my drink, then said, "You've heard of Grover Linden."

"In this town," I said, "you might as well ask me if I know who my father is."

"Great-great-grandfather," he said. "That's his relation to Hugh Paris."

"You're not serious."

Gold merely nodded.

The first time I heard Grover Linden's name I was a fourth-grade student in Marysville. His picture appeared in my social studies book and the caption beneath it identified the broad-faced bearded man as the man who built the railroad. The railroad that connected the west and the east, I learned in high school, took ten years to construct and cost the lives of hundreds as an army of Chinese coolies worked feverishly to break through the Sierras during three of the coldest winters in the nineteenth-century. It was the railroad that raised San Francisco from a backwater village to an international city. It was the railroad from which Grover Linden, who began his adult life as a blacksmith in Utica, derived the wealth that made him the richest man in America.

Linden rose to become a United States senator and bought the Democratic nomination to the presidency. He lost that election, too opulent and corrupt even for that opulent and corrupt era, the Gilded Age. Popular opinion turned against him and he was forced to divest himself of his railroad in a decision by the Supreme Court that I read in my law school anti-trust course. He died in 1920, having nearly lived a century, leaving an immense personal fortune. Almost incidentally, he donated a vast tract of land on the San Francisco peninsula to found the university that bore his name. The first president of the school, Jeremiah Smith, Linden's son-in-law, raided the Ivy League luring entire faculties to California with the promise of unlimited wealth to support their research. In less than a century, Linden University had acquired an international reputation as one of the country's great private schools. The year Gold and I graduated from the law school, the commencement speaker, a United States Supreme Court justice, addressed a distinguished audience that included half the California Supreme Court as well as the sitting governors of three states, all of them alumns. And Linden, statues and paintings of whom were everywhere, lay entombed on the grounds of the school in a marble mausoleum along with his wife, daughter and son-in-law.

"Hugh hasn't told you who his family is?" Gold asked.

"No, not really. I mean — he mentioned money, but I had no idea."

"He didn't tell you his grandfather was Judge Paris?"

"Robert Paris, you mean?"

Gold nodded.

"He told me that, but it's a far cry from someone named Robert Paris to Grover Linden."

"It's complicated," Aaron said. He pulled the slightly soggy cocktail napkin from beneath his drink and got out his pen. "Look," he said. "This is Linden's family tree."

At the top of the tree were Linden and his wife, Sarah. The next generation consisted of their daughter, Allison, who married Jeremiah Smith.

"Then," Gold said, "there were two kids, John Smith and Christina Smith, Linden's grandchildren. Christina married Robert Paris."

"John Smith never married?"

"No," he shrugged. "Linden's descendents aren't prolific. Christina and Robert Paris had two sons, Jeremy and Nicholas." He traced the tree down into that generation. "Nicholas married Katherine Seaton. Hugh is their son."

He tucked his pen back into his coat pocket. I studied the napkin.

"Hugh's the last living descendant of Grover Linden?"

"No, John Smith is very much alive. He controls the Linden Trust," Gold said, referring to the megafund, the income of which supported the university's research which ranged from cancer cures to bigger and deadlier nuclear bombs, with the emphasis on the latter.

"John Smith," I repeated, and, suddenly, it came to me. "He bailed Hugh out of jail."

Gold lifted an eyebrow but said nothing.

"Are there any other descendants?"

"Hugh's father, Nicholas."

"Hugh told me his father was dead."

"He might as well be," Gold said. "Nicholas is locked up in an asylum. A basket case."

"And Hugh's mother, Katherine?"

"The parents divorced twenty years ago. I don't know anything about her."

"You seem to know a lot. Why?"

"Robert Paris is one of my firm's clients," he said glumly. "I'm telling you more than I should have as it is."

"Why tell me this much?"

"For your own good. Hugh's a black sheep."

"Meaning?"

"He has a serious drug problem." I nodded and sipped my beer. "And he's been hospitalized for — I guess you'd call them emotional problems." This I hadn't known but, swallowing my surprise, I nodded again.

Gold looked annoyed, probably having expected shock from me.

"I know about those things."

"And you still plan to see him?"

"I'm not an eighteen-year-old coed," I said, to irritate him further. "What I want to know is your source of information. Robert Paris?"

"Don't ask me to violate a client confidence."

"A strategic attack of ethics, Aaron?"

"Look, Henry, I'm going out on a limb for you. The guy's crazy. He's been threatening his grandfather, calling day and night, writing nutty letters."

"I don't believe you," I said, not without a twinge of anxiety that the allegations were true.

Gold dug into his breast pocket and withdrew a wad of rubber-banded letters. He tossed them at me. "Read them," he commanded.

I leafed through the envelopes. They were postmarked San Francisco, addressed to Robert Paris in Portola Valley but gave no return address. It occurred to me that I did not know what Hugh's handwriting looked like. Clinging to that thread of doubt, I dropped the letters on the table.

"Where did you get these?"

"Afraid to read them?"

"Go to hell," I said, rising, but Gold was on his feet first.

"Fine," he said. "You can shut me out but you have your own doubts about the guy, don't you?" It was a fair statement but I was not inclined to concede the point. "Keep these," he said, indicating the letters. "They make enlightening reading." He drew himself up and walked out. I saw him pass in the window, looking straight ahead. I resisted the impulse to go after him — since I wasn't sure what I wanted to say — and finished my drink. Then, I gathered up the letters and put them in my coat pocket as I rose to leave.

The letters were heavy in my pocket as I walked to my car. There had not been enough time to know Hugh well, particularly since I saw him through the haze of infatuation, but my mind hadn't gone entirely out of commission. Hugh was a troubled man, troubled enough to make threats if not to carry them out. His hatred with his grandfather was fused with his sexual awakening, and his grandfather remained for him a figure who was frightening but seductive. Then, too, the years of drug addiction had taken their toll. Beneath the charm and humor, there was ruin. I saw all this and it made my feeling for him more intense and protective. The letters — and really, I had little doubt he'd written them — complicated matters. They were a sign that the sickness was deeper than I thought, but, even so, he deserved the chance to explain or deny them.

I called Hugh as soon as I got back to my apartment. The phone rang and rang; I pictured the empty room in his house, the phone wailing into the silence. The anxiety I felt in the bar was increasing by the minute and growing more diffuse; fed by emotional and physical exhaustion, it now verged on simple, unthinking panic. Throwing some clothes into a duffle bag, I hurried out to my car and headed for the city.

I was hardly aware of the other traffic on the road or the fading light of late afternoon. By the time I got to Hugh's house it was sunset. The first thing I noticed was that the lights were out. Walking up the stairs to the porch, my hands shook. I searched the door quickly for signs of forced entry but found none. I knocked, much too loudly and for too long. There was no answer. I craned my neck around the side of the porch and looked into the front window. The living room filled with shadowy gray light and the emptiness of the place was an almost physical force. I knew no one was there.

I went back to my car and got in, telling myself he would have to come back eventually. All I had to do was wait. So I waited. The streetlights came on. A police car rolled by. I heard a dog bark. A man and a woman walked by, hand in hand, glancing into my car as they passed. I checked my watch. It was ten. The next time I checked it was nearly six in the morning and I was cramped up behind the steering wheel. My panic had dissipated but, as I looked at the house, it seemed to emanate a kind of deadness.

I went back up the stairs to the porch and knocked on the door. I waited a few minutes, watching the neighborhood awaken to another perfect end of summer day. Defeated, I turned away, went down to my car and left. The drive home seemed endless.

A tall, sandy-haired policewoman was leaning against the wall outside the door to my apartment. She asked me if I was Henry Rios, and, when I agreed that I was, she asked me to step over to her patrol car.

"What's going on, officer?"

"A man died," she said, simply, "and he had your business card on him."

"Who was he?" I asked, as a chill settled along my spine. The bright morning light suddenly seemed stale and unreal.

"We don't know," she said, briskly. "He wasn't carrying a wallet. We'd like you to come down to the morgue and see if you can identify the body."

We went over to the patrol car. Her partner was standing alongside the car drumming his fingers on the roof. He opened the back door for me and I got in. They got into the front and we swept down the quiet street.

"You're a hard man to track down," she said. "We've been trying since last night."

"I was out," I said.

"A bachelor," her partner said, smiling into the rearview mirror. I smiled back.

The coroner was a black man, his dark skin contrasting with his immaculate white frock. He had a round, placid face and his eyes were black and bright. It was a decent face, one that kept its secrets. He led me down a still corridor that stank of chemicals. The officers followed a few steps behind, talking softly. We came to the room and he instructed the police to wait outside. He and I went in.

"They're like kids in here," he said, speaking of the officers. "They get into everything."

I merely nodded and looked around the room. One wall had several metal drawers in it. On the drawers, just below the handles, were slots into which there had been fitted squares of cardboard with names typed on them. There was a row of steel tables, set on casters, lined up against another wall. It was quite cold in the room. A white room. White lights overhead. The coroner moved around quickly and efficiently.

"When did all this happen?" I asked as he put his hand on the handle of a drawer marked John Doe.

"Estimated time of death around 10:30 last night. They found him in San Francisquito Creek just below the footbridge leading out of campus. Drowned."

"In three feet of water?" I asked incredulously.

"We took some blood," he explained quietly. "There was enough heroin in his system to get five junkies off." I opened my mouth but nothing came out. "Are you ready now?"

"Yes."

He pulled at the handle. The drawer came out slowly, exposing first the head, and then the torso, down to the sunken genitals. The coroner stopped and took a step back, as if inspecting death's work.

The elegant body was as white as marble. I could see a dark blue vein running up the length of his arm, and a jagged red mark just beneath his armpit where the needle went in. There were bruises on his chest. His head rested on a kind of pillow. Death had robbed his face of its seductive animation but I recognized him.

"His name is Hugh Paris," I said, and the coroner took a pencil and pad of paper from his pocket and wrote. "His grandfather's name is Robert Paris and he lives somewhere in Portola Valley. I don't know where." I heard the pencil scratching but I could not take my eyes off of Hugh's face.

"Is that it?"

"Yes, that's all."

"The police will want a statement." I looked at the coroner. The dark eyes were impassive but remotely sad as he studied Hugh. "Such a young man. It's a shame."

I agreed that it was a shame and excused myself, hearing, as I left, the drawer slide shut. The two officers were at the far end of the corridor, smoking. They looked up when they saw me and the woman smiled. As I approached, I saw the smile leak from her face. I stopped, ran the back of my hand across my eyes and inspected it. It was wet. I hadn't realized I was crying.

– 4 –

"The coroner says it was an accident."

"The coroner also said he was drugged."

"The guy was a hype. Whaddaya expect?" Torres blew a cloud
of cigar smoke across the small, windowless room, then tilted
back in his swivel chair revealing an enormous stomach that
poured over a heavy metal belt buckle fashioned from the letters
USMC. The desk between us was piled high with papers but he
had cleared enough space for the plastic nameplate that identified him as Samuel Torres, Detective, Homicide.

Torres and I went back a long way. I had once dissected his
testimony on cross-examination in a murder case on which he
was the investigator. He was lucky the jury hadn't hissed him
when he got off the stand. Neither of us had forgotten his
humiliation. Now he studied me with small, dark eyes. On the
wall, above his pitted, jowly face, there was a calendar distributed by some policeman's association. It was a drawing showing
two cops standing against a flowering tree of some kind. They
were dressed in black uniforms, riot helmets on their heads,
jaws adamantly set against the future. Fine art, cop style. That
calendar drawing spoke volumes to me about the cops — they
were menacing and paranoid, and not very bright.

"A hype knows how much he can handle," I said, resuming
my conversation with Torres. It was three in the afternoon, and
I had not been home since I was brought to the morgue that
morning from my apartment.

"Hey, everyone makes a mistake. The guy was just partying. And anyway, counsel" — he said the last word sneeringly — "we got this one figured out."

Now it was my turn to sneer. "Right. You have him wandering around the university at ten at night, shot up with dope, losing his balance, tumbling down the embankment and drowning in three feet of water. It happens every day."

"You're wasting my time," Torres said.

"I don't think that's possible, detective."

"Watch it, Rios. This ain't a courtroom. No judge is gonna take your punches for you."

"I'm terrified."

"Ormes, get him out of here."

The only other person in the office, a woman who had been quietly listening to us, rose from her desk and came over to me. Her nameplate identified her as Terry Ormes, also a homicide detective. She was tall and slender, and she wore a dark blue dress cut so austerely that I had thought it was a uniform at first. She had an open, plain face made plainer by the cut of her hair and the absence of makeup. It wasn't the kind of face that compelled a second look, but if you did look again you were rewarded. Her face radiated intelligence. She studied me for a second with luminous gray eyes.

"Come on, Mr. Rios," she said in a friendly voice, "I'll walk you out."

I shrugged and followed her out of the office, down a bright corridor, past the crowded front desk to the steps of the police station. It was a cool afternoon, cloudy.

"Your colleague's an asshole," I said out of frustration.

"Sam's been around a long time and he's set in his ways. He's not a bad cop, just tired."

The mildness of her reply knocked the air out of my anger. "Well, thanks — Detective."

"Terry," she said, extending her hand.

"I'm Henry," I said, shaking hands.

"I think you're right about Hugh Paris," she said. "I think someone killed him. I just can't figure out who or why."

I looked at her. "Can you talk now?" She nodded. "Let's get a cup of coffee, then." I gestured to a Denny's across the street.

"You look beat," she said, once we were seated in an orange vinyl booth. I took a sip of coffee, tasting nothing but hot.

"It's been a long day and it started at the morgue. Why do you think Hugh was murdered?"

"I was the first one from homicide at the scene this morning," she said. "Are you familiar with the footbridge?"

I said yes. San Francisquito Creek ran along the eastern boundary of the campus at the edge of the wood that fanned out in both directions from the entrance to the school. As the creek flowed north into the bay, it descended, ultimately becoming subterranean as it crept into town. By the time it reached the edge of campus, there was a six-foot embankment down to the water.

Across from the creek was the edge of a shopping center. The footbridge forded the creek at this point, allowing pedestrians access to the shopping center from the walking paths through the wood. The area around the bridge, some of the densest wood on campus, had a bad reputation since it had been the scene of a couple of rapes a few years earlier. It wasn't the kind of place people visited at night.

Terry Ormes was saying, "I was there before they lifted the body out of the water. It was just at dawn and I was watching from the bridge. I swear I saw footprints down there on the bank, and they weren't made by just one pair of shoes."

"How many pairs of shoes?"

"At least two pair. The sand kept the impressions pretty good."

"Anyone take pictures?"

"I went back to my car to radio for a photographer," she said, "but by the time I got back, the paramedics had gone charging down the embankment and pulled him out of the water. They walked all over the place. There was no way to tell."

"That doesn't help much," I said glumly.

She lowered her coffee cup. "That's not all. I walked up that embankment six or seven times. I didn't see anything, not a scrap of clothing or blood or hair or even any broken grass. If Hugh Paris slipped down the embankment, he was awfully careful not to leave any traces behind. And there's one other thing. You saw the body?" I nodded. "Did you see his back?"

"No."

"There were bruises around his shoulders. I think someone held him face down in the water until he drowned."

All I could manage was, "Jesus." There was a long, still moment between us. "Did you tell any of this to Torres?"

"Sure," she said, "but it didn't make it into his report. Like I said, Sam's tired. This one just looked too tough to make out a murder."

I sighed. "Well, he's right, maybe. A jury wouldn't convict a guy of a parking ticket on the evidence we've got."

She gazed at me, coolly. "Why do you care?"

"Hugh was my friend. He told me someone was trying to kill him, but I didn't believe him. Now I owe him the truth, whatever it may be."

"Is that all?"

"You really want to know?"

"No," she said abruptly. "If it's personal, keep it to yourself, but if it's something I can use to investigate, don't hold back. Is that fair?"

"Very fair, detective," I said. "I need more time before I can tell you anything else."

She took out a business card and scribbled a number on the back of it. "My home number," she explained. "This investigation is officially closed, so don't call me at the office." She handed the card to me. "I'll help you if I can."

"Why?"

"I'm a cop," she said, a little defiantly. "We're not all like Sam."

I finished my coffee then found a phone and called the coroner's office to ask when they'd release the autopsy report and their official findings. I was informed that the body had been claimed by the family and there would be no autopsy. The preliminary findings — death by misadventure — would stand. It was hard to get additional information from the sexless bureaucratic whine on the other end of the line but, finally, it told me that Hugh's body had been turned over to his mother, Katherine Paris, who gave a local address and listed the university as her place of employment.

It was dark as I drove home. The tree-lined street where I lived was still and from the windows of my neighbors' houses came the yellow glow of light and domesticity. My own apartment would be dark and chilly. For a moment I considered driving past my building to the nearest bar but I was too tired. I felt the weight of the day and its images like an ache that wracked my brain. Surely we were never meant to live in the appalling circumstances in which we so often found ourselves, alone, fearful, mute. I parked, got out of my car and stood indecisively in the driveway. With whom could I share this loss?

I could think of no one. I walked to my apartment and slipped the key into the lock. I pushed the door open, walked through the living room into the bedroom and lay on the bed, fully clothed. Despite my exhaustion I made myself relive the last day I spent with Hugh, scouring my memory for clues to his death. He'd risen early, put on a tie and blazer. He said he was going out on business and asked me to meet him at the St. Francis around noon. I'd become accustomed to Hugh's solitary comings and goings and once I was satisfied they didn't involve drugs, I relaxed.

I'd arrived at the St. Francis early and had just turned the corner from Geary when I spotted Hugh, his back turned to me, engaged in emphatic conversation with a tall old man. They'd talked for a moment and then the old man got into a silver Rolls.

Uncle John. John Smith.

That's how Hugh referred to the old man, as Uncle John. But he wouldn't tell me anything more and we argued over lunch about it.

"I'm protecting you," I heard him say. Uncle John. That afternoon we made love. And then—

I woke up four hours later, rolled myself over onto my back and sat up. I was certain someone else was in the apartment. I switched on a lamp and made a lot of noise getting out of bed. Then, like a frightened child, I went, noisily, from room to room talking to the darkness as I turned on every light in the apartment. Eventually, I found myself standing in the middle of the living room. I was alone. I stood there for a few minutes, not feeling or thinking anything, not knowing what to do. Then, my stomach, which had been patient all day, roared and demanded food.

I rummaged through the refrigerator coming up with a shriveled apple and a carton of spoiled cottage cheese. In the end, I made my meal out of a bottle of Jack Daniels and a packet of peanuts left over from some long-forgotten airplane trip. I sat down to think. It seemed a waste of time to devise fancy theories about a crime when the evidence was barely sufficient even to establish that a crime had occurred. I believed Hugh had been murdered, but the basis of my belief consisted of Hugh's unsupported assertions and Terry Ormes's unrecorded observations. Clearly, I needed to know more about the Paris family and Hugh's last few months.

The latter I would leave to Ormes — with the resources of the the police department behind her, she could tap into the paper trail that we all generate as we go through life. As for the Paris family and Hugh's relations with it, two names immediately came to mind, Aaron Gold and Katherine Paris. Then I drew a blank. Finally, a third name did occur to me. Grant Hancock. I turned the name over in my mind and mentally wrote beside it, "last resort." Then I poured another drink.

□

The law office of Grayson, Graves and Miller, Aaron Gold's firm, occupied the top three floors of the tallest building in town. A carpeted, wood-paneled elevator whisked me up to the twentieth floor and deposited me in a reception room the size of my entire apartment and considerably better furnished. A middle-aged woman sat behind a semi-circular desk, beneath a Rothko, manipulating the most elaborate phone console I had ever seen. Wading through the carpet, and between the heavy chairs and couches scattered around the room, I approached her and asked for Aaron. She took my measure with a glance and invited me to wait.

Instead, I walked over to a huge globe of the world and spun it. She cleared her throat censoriously and I drifted to the window. The window faced south to the foothills and beyond, where behind rustic stone walls and elaborate electronic alarm systems, the firm's rich clients kept the twentieth century at bay.

Grayson, Graves and Miller was just another weapon in their armory. The receptionist called my name and directed me through the door beside her desk and down the hall. I went through the door and found myself looking down a seemingly endless, blue-carpeted corridor lined with closed doors. I heard a lot of frantic voices coming from behind those doors. The refrigerated air blew uncomfortably as I made my way down the hall looking for Gold's office. This, it occurred to me, was my idea of hell. Just then, a door opened and Gold stepped out and came toward me. The stride was a touch less athletic today, I noticed, and the stomach muscles sagged a bit beneath his elegantly tailored shirt. He was tired around the mouth and eyes and his shaggy hair looked recently slept on.

As we stepped into his office, he instructed his secretary that we were not to be disturbed. On his desk was yesterday's paper turned to the story of Hugh's death. I sat down on a corner of the desk while Aaron stood irresolutely before me.

"I was going to call you," he said.

"I've saved you the trouble." I lifted a corner of the newspaper. "Hugh told me he was in danger of being murdered. I didn't believe him."

Gold said nothing.

"He even told me who the murderer would be, his grandfather, Robert Paris. A client of your firm."

Gold shook his head.

"That can't be true," he said, unconvincingly.

"Then what were you going to call me about?"

Gold wandered over to the liquor cabinet and poured himself some scotch. He held the bottle at me. I shook my head.

"You got Hugh's letters from someone," I continued, "presumably the recepient. If Robert Paris is involved in Hugh's death and you're protecting him, you're already an accessory."

"Don't lecture me about my legal status," Aaron snapped. "I just want to talk."

"I'm listening."

"Judge Paris's account is managed by the two most senior partners in the firm," he began, "but there's enough so that some of it trickles down to the associates. I've done my share of work on that account and I'd heard of Hugh Paris, knew he was the judge's grandson. I'd heard he was bad news," Aaron shrugged. "I really didn't give it much thought."

He sipped his drink.

"Still," he continued, "when you told me he was in jail, I thought that was important enough to mention to one of the partners on the judge's account. I thought we might want to do something for him."

You did, I thought, but said nothing.

"I got the third-degree," Aaron said. "The two partners questioned me for more than an hour. When they were satisfied I wasn't holding back anything they explained to me that Hugh had made threats against the judge's life. I was shown the letters and asked to report back to them anything else that I might learn from you of Hugh's activities."

"And did you?"

"Of course I did," he replied, emptying his glass. "The partners had me convinced that Hugh was dangerous. They told me that he was a drug addict, that his father was crazy. There were disturbing reports from private investigators who'd been hired to keep an eye on him in New York. I not only believed Hugh was a threat to his grandfather but also to you."

I shook my head. "You never met him." Aaron wasn't listening.

"But the more they confided in me," he said, "the stranger it seemed that the judge would go to such lengths and to such expense to keep track of Hugh. It seemed completely out of proportion to any possible threat Hugh may have posed to Robert Paris."

"And now Hugh is dead."

"Yes." He rose from the couch and went back to the liquor cabinet, pouring another drink. "Three days ago I had a meeting with the partners on the Paris account. They asked me a lot of questions about you — questions that contained information they could have got only by having had you followed."

"What kind of questions?"

"They wanted to know the nature of your relationship with Hugh."

"And did you tell them?"

"No, but I think they already knew."

We looked at each other.

"Three days ago," I said, "and the next day we had lunch and you tried to talk me out of seeing Hugh. And that night he was killed."

"I swear I had nothing to do with that," he said.

"But your client — the judge did."

"I don't think it's that simple," Aaron said. "I've been doing some research. Something's going on that goes back a long time and involves a lot of people."

"You're talking in riddles."

"I can't speak more clearly — yet." He looked at me. "I'm going to stay here," his gesture encompassed the entire firm, "until I find out. But I don't want to see you. It's not safe for either of us."

"This is no time to split up," I said.

"They're watching you, Henry. But they're not worried about my loyalties. You're my diversion."

"Why are you doing this, Aaron?"

"I won't be an instrument of crime," he said. "I either have to clear my client of this murder or urge him to turn himself in. That's my obligation."

"Then our interests are different," I said, "because I want justice for my friend."

He nodded. "I'll be in touch, Henry. Wait for my call."

"You have to give me something, Aaron. Something to go on."

"All right," he said. "Robert Paris inherited his wife's estate after she was killed in a car accident. She had a will but she died intestate."

"That doesn't make sense."

"If you can make sense of it," he said, "you'll know who killed Hugh Paris."

I heard the tremor in his voice and I was frightened for both of us.

□

I was sitting on the patio of the student union at the university having left Gold's office an hour earlier. I had come to find Katherine Paris. I stared out across the empty expanse of grass and pavement. Misty light hung from the branches of the trees. A white-jacketed busboy cleared away my breakfast dishes.

School had not yet started for the undergraduates so there was none of their noise and traffic to shatter the stillness. I was thinking about Hugh. The same money that raised this school was responsible for his death. The money was everything and nothing, something that overwhelmed him and which, perhaps, could only be contained by the institution. It had not done Hugh any good, but was merely the background noise against which he played out his unhappiness.

I got up and walked across the plaza to the bookstore. It was a two-story beige box with a red tile roof, a far cry from the excesses of the Old Quad. But then, as the campus moved away from the Old Quad the architecture became purely utilitarian as conspicuous displays of wealth, whether personal or institutional, went out of style. I entered the store and stopped one of the blue-frocked salesclerks, asking where the poetry books were shelved. I was directed to the back wall of the second floor. The poetry books covered a dozen long shelves and it took me a minute to figure out that they were arranged alphabetically.

There had been a brief time in college when I wrote poetry. It was, like most sophomore verse, conceived in the loins rather than the mind. It was a notch better than most such verse, perhaps, but it was no loss to literature when I stopped writing. My brush with poetry, however, left me with a permanent respect for those who wrote it well. Seeing familiar names again, Auden, Frost, Richard Wilbur, took me back to sunny autumn afternoons when I sat in my dorm room writing lame couplets.

Katherine Paris had published a half-dozen slender volumes over the past twenty years and one thick book of collected poems. Each book was adorned with the same photograph I had seen at Hugh's house and beneath it was the same paragraph of biographical information. She was born in Boston, graduated from Radcliffe, took a master's degree from Columbia and currently divided her time between Boston and San Francisco. Her work had won the National Book Award and been nominated for the Pulitzer Prize. She had been translated into twelve languages — they were listed — and had once been mentioned by T.S. Eliot who found her work elliptical. Nothing about a crazy husband and a homosexual son; apparently, that information was private.

I struggled with about a dozen of her poems before I saw Eliot's point. Her work was indeed elliptical, she left out everything that was essential, including logic and meaning. Her words neither described nor observed things. They were just words scattered across the page. This was braininess of the highest order, the verbal equivilant of the white canvas passed off as a painting; so abstract that to have expected some sense from it would have insulted the artist. As my attention wandered from the poems, it seemed to me that I was being watched. I closed the book and looked around. The boy standing next to me quickly directed his attention to his feet.

He wore a baggy pair of khaki shorts rolled up at the bottom over a long sinewy pair of legs. He had on a white sweatshirt with a red paisley bandana tied around his neck and a small button with the lambda — the symbol of gay liberation — on it. He had a round cherubic face, short hair of an indeterminate dark color. He looked about twenty. He raised his eyes at me and I realized that I was being cruised, not spied on.

"Hello," I said, pleasantly.

Pointing at the book in my hand he said, "I took a creative writing course from her last quarter." Almost as an afterthought, he added, "My name is Danny."

"Henry," I said. "Did you like the course?"

"Actually," he confided, pushing his hair with slender fingers, "she's a good poet but a very neurotic woman."

"Don't the two go together?"

"No," he said, "I reject the notion of the doomed artist. I mean, look at Stevens, he sold insurance and Williams was a doctor."

"Sorry," I said, "It's been a long time since I read poetry. Who are Stevens and Williams?"

He looked slightly shocked. "Wallace Stevens? William Carlos Williams?" I shook my head. Looking at me intently he said, "Aren't you a student? A grad student maybe?"

"I'm a lawyer and my interest in Katherine Paris is professional, not literary."

"A lawyer," he repeated as though describing a virus. "Don't lawyers wear suits when they're working?" I was wearing a pair of jeans and a black polo shirt.

"Not on house calls," I replied. "Where can I find Mrs. Paris?"

"Third floor, English department in the Old Quad. I'll walk you there if you like, okay?"

"Sure, just let me pay for the book."

Between the bookstores and the Old Quad I learned quite a bit about Danny's tastes in poetry, his life and his plans as well as receiving a couple of gently veiled passes. I steered the conversation around to Katherine Paris.

"She had this great lady persona," he was saying, "but don't cross her."

"You did?"

"Anyone with any integrity does sooner or later. Her opinions are set in stone."

"Not writ in water?"

"That's Shelley. That was pretty good. Anyway, she doesn't let you forget who has the power." We had reached the English department. He smiled at me, sunnily. "What do you want with her anyway?"

"Her son was killed on campus a couple of days ago. He was a friend of mine. I want to ask her some questions."

"You mean the guy that they found in the creek?" I nodded. "That's too bad. Was he a good friend?"

I reached out and touched the button on his chest. "We were good friends."

His look said, "And here I've been cruising you." Aloud, he said, "You must think I'm a real jerk."

"How could you have known?" I asked, reasonably. "And thanks for the help." We shook hands, he a little awkwardly and I remembered how rare the gesture was among students. "The poem with the phrase writ in water, that was about Keats, wasn't it?"

"Yes," he said. "Shelley wrote it when Keats died. He called it Adonais." He started to say something else, thought better of it, smiled again and walked away. I watched him go and then turned and climbed up the stairs to the third floor.

□

Katherine Paris did not look like a woman anyone ever called mother. Her small feet were encased in gold slippers and she wore a flowing white caftan that obliterated any sign of a body beneath it. The string of blue beads around her neck was probably lapis lazuli. It was the only jewelry she wore. Her face had the false glow of a drinker but none of a drinker's soft alcoholic bloat. It was a hard angular face I saw as I entered her office; deeply wrinkled, deeply intelligent. She instructed me to sit down. I sat. She continued writing.

The walls of the office were bare. The curtains were drawn against the afternoon light and the only source of light was her desk lamp. She worked at an elegant writing table whose spindly legs hardly seemed able to bear the weight of the books piled on top. At length, she looked up at me from beneath half-glasses evidently surprised to find that I was still there.

I introduced myself, to her obvious pleasure, as an admirer of her work. She accepted the volume of her collected poems and signed it for me.

"How were you introduced to my poetry?" she asked. Her voice was a low, whisky rumble.

"Your son, Hugh," I replied and, at once, the pleasure vanished. Her eyes narrowed.

"I see. Tell me, Mr. Rios, which of my poems is your favorite? Or have you actually opened this — brand new book?"

"In fact I have, Mrs. Paris, but you're right, I didn't come here to discuss them. I'm a lawyer."

"Is that a threat?"

"Mrs. Paris, I was Hugh's friend—

"Hugh was rather generous in that regard. He had altogether too many friends. Were you one of his — special friends?" she asked archly.

"I cared for Hugh," I said.

"Mr. Rios," she said, mockingly, "spare me the homosexual sentimentality. What is it you want from me?"

"I believe Hugh was murdered. I'm not sure by whom but the

first thing to do is determine the exact cause of death. The body was moved before an autopsy—"

"That's enough," she said. "You walk in from nowhere, tell me someone killed my son and ask permission to cut open his body?" These last words were delivered in a tone of rising incredulousness. "Just who the hell are you? One of his boyfriends? Do you think there's money for you in this?"

Unable to suppress my hostility, I said, "Mrs. Paris, I sympathize with your deep grief, however, I'm talking about a crime."

"My deep grief? Getting himself killed was the most unselfish thing Hugh ever did. As for the body, it was cremated yesterday. As for crimes, Mr. Rios, you're now trespassing and in one minute I'm going to call campus security and have you thrown out." She picked up the phone.

"Why was he cremated?" I asked, rising.

"That is not your business," she said, "now get out."

"Thank you for your time, Mrs. Paris." She put the phone down and went back to her writing.

□

Sitting on my patio an hour later, I finished a gin-and-tonic, watched clouds move in from the ocean and counted up my leads. They amounted to about nothing. There were Hugh's allegations against his grandfather and the coincidence of his death under odd circumstances. Gold knew more than he was saying, but either he could not say any more or really believed that our interests were sufficiently different for him not to confide in me. Katherine Paris was a dead end. I needed something tangible. It seemed to me that Hugh Paris moved through life like a nomad, using life up as he lived it, and leaving very little behind.

And then I remembered the letters. They were still in the pocket of the coat I had worn three days earlier. I finished my drink and went to the closet to retrieve them. Even as I spread them out on my desk a voice within begged me not to read them. I was afraid of what they might contain. I made myself another drink and circled my desk, vaguely, looking at them — thirteen in all, arranged from the earliest, in June, to the most recent, only a couple of weeks earlier. Finally, I sat down and started reading.

They were not exactly the rantings of a lunatic. On the other hand, there was little in them that could be called civilized discourse. Mostly, they were excruciatingly detailed invective of a psychosexual nature — literate but profoundly disturbed. I refolded the last letter and tucked it back into its envelope. It seemed impossible these could come from Hugh, but the details told. I said to myself that I was now his advocate, not his lover, and an advocate accepts revelations about his client that would send the lover running from the room. It's part of the masochism of being a criminal defense lawyer to want to know the worst, in theory so the worst can be incorporated into the defense, but in actuality to confirm a blighted view of humanity. If I believed that people are basically good, I would have gone into plastics. People are basically screwed-up and often the best you can do for them is listen, hear the worst and then tell them it's not so bad.

It wasn't so bad, Hugh, I said, silently. I've seen worse. And the letters contained solid information. Hugh believed his grandfather was responsible for the deaths of his grandmother and his uncle, Jeremy. He also accused the judge of imprisoning his father, Nicholas, in an asylum. Finally, he accused the judge of depriving him of his lawful inheritence. There wasn't much elaboration since, obviously, Hugh expected his grandfather to understand the allusions. It wasn't evidence but it was something. A lead. A theory. Hugh's death was part of a cover-up of earlier murders. All right, so it was melodramatic. Most crime is.

I collected my thoughts and called Terry Ormes. Her crisp, friendly voice was a relief after the dark muttering voice of the letters. I told her, briefly, editing out the lurid details, what the letters contained.

"That's still not much," she said.

"Well, it's something. Apparently, Hugh's grandmother and his uncle were killed up near Donner Pass on interstate 80 about twenty years ago. Can you contact the local police agency in the nearest town up there with a hospital?"

"Sure," she said, "but if it happened on 80, it was probably a CHP case. What am I asking for?"

"Everything you can find out about the circumstances of their deaths. Any reports, death certificates, anything. And find out anything you can about Hugh's life the last six months. Rap sheets, DMV records, any kind of paper."

"Call me in two days," she said. "What will you do?"

"I have one other card to play," I said. "I'll be in touch."

The line went dead. I gathered up the letters and buried them beneath a pile of papers in the bottom drawer of my desk. I closed and locked it. For a long time I sat, nursing my drink, thinking about the hole where my heart had been.

— 5 —

The next morning I sat down to dial a number I'd not called in four years. The receptionist I reached announced the name of the law firm in the hushed tones appropriate to old money. I gave her the name I wanted and waited the couple of minutes it took to work through the various intermediaries until a deep unhurried male voice spoke.

"Grant Hancock here."

"Grant, this is Henry Rios."

There was the slightest pause before breeding won out and he said, "Henry, it's been a long time."

"Four years, at least."

"Are you in the city?"

"No, I'm calling from my apartment. Grant, I need your advice."

"Surely you don't need the services of a tax lawyer on what you make with the public defender."

"I'm not a P.D. anymore," I replied, "and what I want to talk about is death, not taxes."

"Anyone's in particular?"

"Yes, Hugh Paris. I thought since you're both — well, old San Francisco stock — that you might have known him."

"Indeed I did," Grant said slowly. "How well did you know him?"

"Well enough to think that he was murdered." The line buzzed vacantly. "Grant? Are you still there?"

"Yes," he said. "I don't want to discuss this over the phone. Can you come up here tonight?"

"About nine?"

"Fine. I'm still at the same place. You know the way." I agreed that I did.

"Henry, did Hugh mention me? Is that why you called?" His voice was, for Grant, agitated.

"No, he never said anything about you. It was my own idea to call. I know how thick the old families are with each other."

"I knew him a long time ago," Grant said in a far-off voice, and then stopped himself short. "I'll talk to you tonight." The line went dead.

Grant Hancock, along with Aaron Gold, had been one of my two closest friends at law school. His name was the amalgamation of two eminent San Francisco families and he grew up in a mansion in Pacific Heights. He was one of those San Francisco aristocrats who, for all their culture and worldliness, never move a psychological inch from the tops of their hills. Among those families that gave the city its reputation for insularity, "provincial" was a compliment.

In the normal course of existence, I would never have met someone like Grant since his world was far removed from mine and hardly visible to the untrained eye. Its tribesmen recognized each other by certain signs and signals meaningless to the outsider. However, Linden University was an extension of that world and the law school was a kind of finishing school from which he entered a law practice so leisurely and refined that it would have befitted one of Henry James's languid heros.

Grant cultivated a certain languor and part of it was real, growing out of a sense of belonging that was deep and unshakable. Part of it was an act, a way of masking real passion and a strong if confused decency. His decency was as simple as the desire to treat everyone fairly and civilly but it was undercut by his knowledge that, from his position of privilege, he could afford to act decently at no cost to himself. He wondered how he would treat others had he not been so privileged, and, I think, he assumed the worst about himself.

The fact that he was gay added to his confusion because acknowledging his homosexuality was an opportunity to take a moral risk and he passed it up. He rigidly separated his personal and professional lives and spent great amounts of energy policing the border between them. And for all that, I had once loved him and he had loved me. There had even been a time when it appeared that we might live together, openly, but that time came and passed, and he could not bring himself to do it. We drifted apart, he back to his hill and I back to real life.

I was thinking about all this as I finished dressing and made a pot of coffee. There was something of Grant in Hugh Paris as if Hugh had been a version of Grant more comfortable with himself and more distant from that insular world of old money and unchanging attitudes. I let the comparison lie. There was work to be done.

The weather was beautiful, almost cruelly so, I thought as I walked across the parking lot to the courthouse. The deep and broad blue sky and the dazzling morning sun which should have looked down upon an innocent landscape instead shone above cramped suburban cities and cramped suburban lives. The sunlight brushed the back of my neck as if it were fingers wanting me only to stop for a moment and do nothing but breathe and be grateful that I was alive. Another time, I thought as I pushed open the glass door to the courthouse.

I walked up the stairs to the clerk's office on the second floor. Telephones screeched and voices rose in frustration at the service counter. This was the place where court records relating to criminal cases were kept. By the time I got a sullen clerk's attention, I had forgotten the weather and gratitude was the farthest thing from my mind. Having already located the case number on a master index, I ordered the court docket on Hugh's case to see what had happened to it. Fifteen minutes later, the docket was regurgitated from the bowels of the bureaucracy by the same clerk, who warned me three times not to remove the file from the room.

I went over to the reading counter and flipped through the pages of the docket. The criminal charges filed against Hugh the day after his arrest were possession of PCP, being under the influence of PCP and resisting arrest — all misdemeanors. His arraignment had been set for a week after his release from jail. On that day, he appeared through his attorney, Stephan Abrams, and the D.A. moved to dismiss all charges against him. The court granted the motion and that was the end of the case. I made a mental note of the D.A.'s name: Sonny Patterson, an old courtroom adversary. I had the docket copied and went down the hall to the office of the District Attorney.

Sonny Patterson rattled the docket sheet and dropped it on his desk. He took a drag from his cigarette, scattering ashes on his pale green shirt and bright orange tie. Hick was written all over his puffy potato face, but it was an act, like his carefully mismatched clothes. He got juries to like him by letting them think that they were smarter than he. But Sonny had a mind for detail and one that made connections. A good mind. Evasive when circumstances required evasion. He was being evasive now.

"Come on Henry, I handle twenty cases a day in the arraignment court. You're talking a thousand cases ago."

"It's not every day that you dismiss a three-count complaint involving drugs and resisting arrest."

"Misdemeanors," he replied disdainfully.

"Being under the influence carries a mandatory thirty day jail sentence."

"So?" he said, shrugging. "With good time/work time figured in you're out in twenty."

"That's still twenty days longer in county than I'd care to spend."

"I know your position on determinate sentencing, counsel," he said stiffly.

I held up my palms. "Sorry," I said. "I didn't come here to debate the point. I just want to know why you dumped the case."

"What was the defendant's name again?" he drawled in a vaguely Southern accent. Another affectation. The furthest south Sonny had ever been was Castroville.

"Hugh Paris," I replied.

"Isn't he the guy they pulled out of the creek about a week back?"

"The same."

"You know him pretty well?"

"Yes," I said.

"The papers say it was an accident."

"So do the cops."

"I know," he said, "I had Torres up here to tell me about it. He mentioned — in passing — that you identified the body." He leaned forward on his desk. "Do you know anything about this man's death that the police don't know?"

Police, I thought. Did he mean the cops? Any moment now he'll be calling them peace officers. Aloud I said, carefully, "I don't know anything about Hugh's death the cops don't know. I just added up the information differently."

"So did I," he said, picking up the phone and pushing a button. He reeled off a string of numbers into the receiver. A couple of minutes later there was a knock on the door and his secretary entered with a thick file. Hugh's name was written across the outside of the manila folder. She put the file on the desk and Sonny flipped through the arrest report to the three sheets of yellow paper on which the complaint appeared. He turned the last sheet over to some writing. This was the alibi, so-called because every time a D.A. dismissed a case he was required to set out his reasons on the back of the complaint in the event someone — like a cop or irate citizen — took exception to the dismissal down the road.

"Insufficiency of the evidence," Sonny said, lifting his face from the sheet.

"That's meaningless. What was the problem?"

"The alleged PCP cigarette was analyzed by the crime lab and came back as creatively rolled oregano, dipped in ether to give it the right smell. Mr. Paris's pusher misled him. Street justice, I guess."

"And the other charges?"

"We won't pursue the under the influence charge unless the defendant was examined by a doctor at the time of his arrest. The cops didn't do that."

"What about the resisting arrest count?"

"That was plain, old-fashioned contempt of cop. A little chickenshit charge. Not worth the paper it was written on." He glanced at the complaint with an expression almost of distaste. I wasn't surprised by his reaction. The D.A.'s know better than anyone what cops can be like — touchy, hostile, self-righteous.

"Have you ever heard of that lawyer, Abrams, before?"

"Nope. He's not a local. He's got himself a fancy address up in the city. You want it?"

I nodded.

He scrawled an address on a sheet of legal paper and pushed it across the desk.

"Thanks," I said, rising to go. "You don't think Hugh's death was an accident, either, do you?"

"If I did," he said, suddenly grim, "I wouldn't have given you the time of day."

"Then why are you?"

"The cops botched this one," he said. "I know it, but I can't prove it. I've already beefed Torres but even if they reopen the investigation now, the trail's cold. You seem to know something about this case. Better you than no one. Good luck and remember," he said, as I opened the door, "you're an officer of the court."

"Meaning?"

"If you find out who did it, let me know the bastard's name. He won't get away with it."

But so often criminals do, I nearly said, but I kept the thought to myself.

At the end of the day I drove to San Francisco on highway 280, the serpentine road that wound through the foothills behind the posh peninsula suburbs and within view of the hidden houses of the rich. The twisted eucalyptus trees stood high and elegantly on those hills and the air was moist with the fragrance of their leaves. Deer grazed those hills and now and then a jeep went flying along the dirt roads with no apparent destination. A line of horses appeared on the horizon and then disappeared behind a clump of oak.

I was passing through some of the wealthiest communities in the country, and the only sign of money was its absence. The developer's hand was stayed from these hills and woods to perpetuate a view of California as it had existed a hundred years earlier. Even the Southern Pacific commuter train, whose whistle I heard in the distance, was a subsidized prop, reminding listeners of the pristine age before Henry Ford gave wheels to the masses. A hundred years earlier, Grover Linden raised monuments to his wealth, but his heirs bought privacy, the ultimate luxury. Judge Paris lived somewhere in those hills, as safe as money could make him. Like God, he moved a finger and the sparrow fell. To him, a little death. But not to me. I floored the accelerator as if physical speed could make time move faster. I would bring this death home to him, whatever it took.

I followed a curve in the road and when I looked up, the darkened skyline burst across the rose-colored sky of dusk, vaguely Oriental in shape and pattern and decidedly sinister. This was the first time I had returned to San Francisco since Hugh's death. Those untroubled summery days seemed far more remote than a mere ten days ago. I exited near the Civic Center and came up Market, now nearly deserted as downtown emptied, toward the bay. For all its magnificence the city seemed shabby to me as little gusts of winds kicked up scraps of newspaper and blew them across the street and the bag ladies stood shapelessly in front of dark windows muttering invectives. It would be cold later. I had not thought to bring a coat.

Stephan Abrams's office was on the fifth floor of a highrise on Montgomery Street. Having called him earlier, I followed his directions and got to his office a few minutes before I was expected. His secretary told me he was on the phone and asked me to sit and wait. I took a look around the office. Chrome-and-leather furniture, off-white walls, industrial gray carpeting, an unnumbered Miro lithograph; all the indicia of unspectacular success. He entered the room and confirmed my image of him.

Abrams was bulky but not fat. He had sharply etched features, a receding hairline he made no attempt to disguise, and eyes that shone from deep within their sockets. He wore a dark gray suit, a white shirt, red silk tie. He looked solid, not one to start a fight but not one to run from a fight either. The perfect all-purpose family lawyer. We shook hands. His grip, predictably, was firm.

"Mr. Rios?" he said. "I'm sorry to make you come up so late in the day but I was booked solid."

"That's fine. I have another appointment a little later."

"Oh? Well, then, there's no problem, is there? You said something over the phone about a client we had in common."

"Yes, Hugh Paris."

"Maggie," he said to his secretary, "why don't you go on home, now. I'll close up here. Step into my office Mr. Rios."

I went into his office and he followed me in, closing the door behind him. There were the usual framed degrees on the wall, one from Berkeley and another from Hastings Law School, full of seals and flourishes; a little vulgar, I thought. Abrams stepped over to a small roll-top desk against a wall, fiddled with the lock and opened it to reveal a bar. He motioned me to one of the two armchairs in front of a large plain desk in the center of the room. Without asking, he poured two glasses of scotch, Chivas Regal, and carried them over. He sat down in the other chair and handed me a glass.

"So," he said, "Hugh Paris. At what point did you represent him?"

"I didn't, actually. I offered but he turned me down. Then you picked up the case and got the charges dismissed."

"It wasn't hard, considering the lab report. Your cops have itchy fingers down there, but then that's true of cops in most college towns when it comes to drugs."

"The voice of experience?"

"I was a P.D. too, in Berkeley, back in the 'sixties." He took a healthy swallow of his drink. I swilled mine around in my glass, to be sociable. I hate scotch. "But the fires burn out."

"You're doing well."

"I have no complaints," he said. "So, what's on your mind, Mr. — look, do you have a first name? Mine's Steve." He smiled engagingly. I was beginning to dislike him.

"Henry," I said. "Did Hugh hire you?"

"I was retained on his behalf."

"By whom? Robert Paris? Aaron Gold?"

"I have to claim the privilege, counsel. But if you speak frankly, then perhaps I can, too."

"Hugh was murdered," I said. "That's to the point, isn't it?"

"Brutally," he replied, smiling. "Do you have any evidence to support your assertion?"

"None that I can share with you." His eyebrows shot up. "But it seems to me that someone who cared enough to hire a lawyer on his behalf might also care enough to assist me in finding his murderer."

"Anything you say to me, Henry, I assure you will reach the right ears."

"I don't deal with middlemen," I said, tasting the scotch.

"Then why did you come here? To insult me?"

"To give your client a message," I said.

"A message, Henry?" he asked softly. "If you want to deliver a message, I suggest UPS. Their rates are lower than mine."

"Tell your client I know who killed Hugh Paris. The police are cooperating and it's just a matter of time before we nail him. He's not safe. And neither are you. You may not answer my questions but you'll answer to a subpoena and, if you're helping to cover up a crime, I'll have you brought up before the Bar."

"Get out of here, Henry, before I throw you out," he said, rising. "Now."

I stood up. "All right. Thank you for your time — Steve. And here's my card." I flicked it on the desk.

I shut the door behind me, and stood outside waiting to see if he picked up the phone. He didn't. I went out into the street. I'd blown it. My purpose in coming to Abrams was to find out for whom he worked and the extent of his relationship to Hugh. Instead, I'd implied misconduct on his part and threatened him. Those were courtroom tactics, not the way to handle an investigation. But then, I'd been thrown out of a number of offices during this investigation. I seemed to be making people uncomfortable. That was some progress. Now, if I could only get them to talk. I set off in the darkness to find Grant Hancock.

□

Grant lived in a twenty-eighth floor condominium in a building that rose above Embarcadero Plaza. I walked there from Abrams's office through the early evening. Seagulls squawked overhead as I approached the blue awning that marked the entrance. A doorman stood just outside the double glass doors. He wore a blue blazer over gray flannel trousers. I noted the bulge beneath his jacket where he strapped his holster. It was an odd neighborhood for a luxury high-rise, but there were spectacular views of the bay from the condos and, at night, it was as quiet in the streets as a graveyard. In the noisy, cramped city in which new construction was constantly obliterating someone's view, peace and a vista of Sausalito from the living room were reason enough to pay the toney prices for a few hundred square feet of condo.

I identified myself to the doorman and he called up to Grant's apartment. A moment later I boarded a dimly-lit elevator that carried me to the twenty-eighth floor.

I rang the bell and he opened the door. Behind him, in the darkness, candles were burning, and his window framed the bridge and the lights of Marin blazing across the bay. He still wore the slacks from his suit and a button-down shirt the shade of pearl, purchased, no doubt, from one of those men's shops that sell to you only if your great-grandfather had an account with them. The three top buttons of his shirt were undone, revealing a patch of tanned and expensively maintained flesh. His sandy hair was clipped short above his ears and the handsome, expressionless face was as mysterious and self-contained as ever. He smelled of bay rum, and his clear blue eyes took me in with a long detached look. I could see myself in that look; disheveled, thin, dark beneath the eyes and getting grayer, liquor on my breath. I heard, for the first time, music playing softly in the room, guitar and flute.

"Come in, Henry," he said stepping back. I took it all in and smiled. The room was a joke. The candles were set in a pair of silver candlesticks atop an orange crate. There were some pillows stacked against the wall and an elaborate stereo system but no other furnishings. There was, I remembered, a mattress on a box spring in the bedroom and a butcher block table and two chairs in the kitchen. The refrigerator was apt to be stocked with wine, fruit juices, vitamins, some apples and cheese. The kitchen shelves contained a few mismatched plates of heirloom china and beautiful old wine glasses. He was holding one in his hand. The years had faded for a moment and all my feeling for him came back with an intensity that made my heart pound. And then he took a step and the feeling passed as quickly as it had come.

"I see the decorator hasn't been in yet," I said, more edgily than I'd intended.

Grant shrugged. "When I get lonely for furniture I go to my father's house. A glass of wine? Or do you want to stick to whiskey?"

"Wine," I said. "I was drinking scotch with a lawyer."

"A seemingly innocent pursuit," he observed drily, pressing a glass into my hand. "You're awfully thin, Henry. Still forgetting to eat?"

"As always. You look — very well, Grant."

Aloud he said, "Thank you," but he was thinking something else. Bad feelings have a life of their own.

I wanted desperately to say something that would wipe away the stain from our last, angry conversation four years earlier but for me that was all history. I had lost the scent of the emotions that led to the breakup. I had almost forgotten that I was the one who stopped returning calls. I could only think of how well he looked and how it was good to see him.

He sat on the floor, cross-legged. Candlelight blazed through his hair. Theatrical, I thought, but effective. I lowered myself to the floor until we were face to face. "I wanted to ask you about Hugh," I began, tentatively.

"Yes, of course."

"What did you know about him?"

He shrugged. "The Paris family is peninsula and seldom ventures up to the city. I didn't really know Hugh until we were undergrads at Yale. He was younger than I by a couple of years and I took him under my wing." He looked into his wine glass. "I was in love with him," he added simply.

"What happened?"

"Hugh was eighteen and not out of the closet. Neither was I, for that matter. He was tactful enough to overlook my infatuation. We behaved toward each other," he said, suddenly bitter, "like perfect young gentlemen. And at night I lay in bed praying to God to make me different or kill me or, preferable to either, put Hugh beside me."

"You never told me any of this."

"It was ancient history by the time I met you and, besides, I hadn't seen or heard from Hugh in years. Not until about six months ago when I ran into him on the streets. He saw me and tried to slip by but I stopped him. He wasn't particularly friendly but he agreed to have a drink with me that night."

"And did you?"

"Yes, and he spent the night here." A twinge of jealousy constricted my chest for a second. "It was nothing like I'd imagined it would be when I was nineteen," Grant added. "It wasn't memorable and yet—" he poured wine into his glass from the bottle beside him — "I've thought of him almost every day since then. He's one of those people who live less in your memory than your imagination. Like a symbol."

"Of what?" I asked.

"I suppose it's different for everyone who knew him," Grant replied. "For me, he was a symbol of being young and unknowing."

"I've never thought that was an enviable state."

"No? Then maybe life has spared you some of the things I know about."

"I don't think I've been spared much of life's nastiness," I said, "but I don't take it personally. And as for Hugh, I preferred the flesh-and-blood human to the symbol. Tell me, what do you know about the judge?"

"What does anyone know about Robert Paris? The poor boy who made good by marrying into the right family. My father thinks he's the ultimate nouveau riche, but no one denies that he's a brilliant and ruthless man. Of course, that was before the stroke. Now I hear he's half-dead but he hasn't actually been seen in town for months."

"What stroke?"

"He had a series of strokes about a year ago. Since then, he's stayed up on the Linden estate in Portola Valley. He sees no one, and no one sees him."

"What about a man named John Smith?" I asked.

"Are we going to explore every branch of the Linden family tree?" Grant asked mockingly.

"Hugh saw him the day he was killed."

"Well, he is Hugh's great-uncle," Grant replied. "So surely there's nothing unusual about Hugh having seen him."

"I don't know. Is there? What kind of man is John Smith?"

"He's a stuffy old zillionaire," Grant said, "nominally a banker but only in the sense that he owns banks. He's Robert Paris's brother-in-law and controls the other half of the Linden fortune. He and the judge don't get along."

"Really? Do you know that as a fact?"

"Good Lord, Henry, half of the city knows that as a fact."

"Then he's someone Hugh might have gone to for help."

"Help for what?"

"I don't know. I'd like to talk to him though."

"It's easier to see the Pope," Grant said, "and probably more fun."

"What do you mean?"

"Smith is a recluse. You'd never get past the palace guard."

"Could you?"

"I'd have to know why I'm trying."

"I think Robert Paris had Hugh murdered."

Grant sipped his wine. "You're crazy," he remarked cheerfully. "Smith would throw you out the minute you uttered those words." Grant shook his head. "Sorry, I can't help you."

He finished his wine and set the glass down on the floor.

"I'm perfectly serious, Grant."

"That's your forte," he said, "but even so you don't go to someone like John Smith to accuse a member of his family of homicide. That's what the police are for."

"They're not interested."

"Then perhaps you should take your cue from them," he said, rising. "I'm going out to get some dinner. Want to join me?"

"I can't tonight, but I'll take a rain check."

"Suit yourself," he said. "I'll call you."

Rising to leave I said, "It was good to see you again, Grant."

A smile, at once cynical and tender, flickered across his lips. "What amazes me most about you," he said, "is your sincerity."

"I'm afraid that it's my only social skill."

"Good night, Henry," he said, letting me out.

I stepped out of Grant's building, passing the doorman who acknowledged my departure with the slightest of nods. I had parked down by the piers on Embarcadero and had walked, first to Abrams' office and then to see Grant. Now as I returned to my car, walking beneath the freeway, the streets around Embarcadero Plaza were deserted. It was only the racket from the freeway and the lumbering noise of the buses as they screeched to a halt at the nearby bus yard that gave an illusion of activity.

It was the road noise that kept me from making out my name the first time it was shouted by a voice behind me. The second time I heard it distinctly, stopped, and turned around. A man, my height but considerably more muscular, hurried toward me. He wore tight levis and a leather bomber jacket over a white t-shirt. As he stepped beneath a streetlight, I saw he was carrying something in his right hand. A gun. Aimed at my stomach.

"Henry," he said in a friendly voice, "I've been shouting at you for the last block." His dark hair was cut short and he wore a carefully clipped moustache. He was good-looking in an anonymous sort of way. A Castro clone.

"I don't think I know you," I said.

"Well, we're going to be good friends before the night is over."

He kept the gun on me while he raised his left hand in the air and motioned toward us. A moment later a car — black, Japanese, four-door, with its lights out and no license plate — crept up beside us. Two other men were in the front seat and one in the back. The two in the front and my friend with the gun were not only dressed identically but, as far as I could see, might have been a set of triplets. The man in the back seat differed from the others only in that he was a blond. He stepped out of the car and approached us.

"Hello, Henry. Just relax and do what you're told and everything will be fine."

"Sure," I said, as the car came up directly behind me.

The blond reached into his back pocket and pulled out a black bandana, of the kind allegedly used by some gay men to indicate their sexual specialties. I didn't think that he was signaling me for a date. Smiling, he brought the bandana over my eyes and tied it at the back of my head.

"Put your hands out, please," he said.

I put my hands out slowly. They were bound with rough twine. I was led by the arm into the back seat, where I was wedged between the two men. Lest I forget who was in charge, the dark-haired man pushed the nozzle of the gun against my side, just below my ribs.

The motor started and the car jumped forward. It was pretty quiet outside, so I assumed we were traveling on the periphery of the city. I had no sense of time. Finally, we stopped and the only noise I heard was the sound of the sea as someone unrolled a window and the wind swept in.

It occurred to me that I was about to be killed. I wondered if it would hurt. I wondered if there was an after-life. I supposed that I was about to find out. It was too bad I hadn't gone to dinner with Grant.

"Who sent you?" I asked.

A voice that I recognized as belonging to the blond said, reasonably, "Don't ask questions you don't expect answers to."

My arms were pulled out in front of me. I felt something cold and liquid dabbed at the inside of my arm at my elbow. The smell of alcohol filled the car.

"Nice biceps," the blond said. "You lift weights, Henry?"

"No," I said. "It's heredity."

"You're lucky then," he replied. "I have to lift pretty hard to stay in shape."

The needle hit me with a shock, and I jerked my arms back.

"Steady," the dark-haired man said, holding the gun against my neck. "Stay cool."

"What is it?" I asked.

"We have some questions for you," the blond replied. "This will make it easier for you to answer them."

Minutes, or hours, passed. My tongue felt heavy in my mouth. Things stopped connecting in my head. I struggled to stay awake but it was like trying to keep my exhausted body afloat in a warm sea. It was so much easier just to give up and go under.

"Sodium pentothal," I muttered in a voice that I vaguely recognized as my own. "Truth serum."

"Very impressive," the blond said. "Now relax."

"It doesn't work," I murmured, half to myself. "Results aren't admissible in court. I won't tell you — anything I — don't want to—"

"Quiet now," one of them was saying. I couldn't tell which anymore. "Rest. Later we'll talk."

I heard a roaring in my ears that was either the ocean or the sound of my blood.

— 6 —

Something scampered across my ankles. I opened my eyes in time to watch a rat's tail disappear between one of the two garbage cans I was wedged between. It was still dark. There was a wall behind me, a street-lamp far away, and even more distant, the noise of traffic. My head felt like glass, as if the slightest unplanned move would shatter it. I turned my wrist and slowly brought my watch to my face. It was one-thirty. I had left Grant's apartment just before ten — three and a half hours lost. I tried to remember. We had driven around a lot and someone asked me a lot of questions but I couldn't remember what had been said or whether I'd responded. And then I passed out. And now I was awake.

Sort of.

I lifted myself up and found that I was standing in an alley that dead-ended into a brick wall. At the other end, I saw a light and started moving toward it. The light seemed to move away and I kept running into things, trash cans, piles of boxes, the wall. This is not a dream, I told myself, though the atmosphere was as fetid as a nightmare. Finally, I reached the lamp-post and hugged it, closing my eyes and waiting for things to stop spinning. When I looked again, everything was more or less still as I tried to get my bearings.

There was a wide, dimly lit street beside me and warehouses all around. The spire of the Transamerica pyramid, surrounded by the other downtown skyscrapers, loomed ahead of me. Judging by distance, I concluded that I was somewhere south of Market. I made my way up to the first intersection and read the street signs, Harrison at Third; one block south of Folsom and about eight blocks east of the gay bars where I might find help. I headed north to Folsom and turned left, feeling worse with each step as I became more conscious of my nausea and my aching body. The street was full of shadows and silences, and the darkness seemed unending. Had I been in less pain, I would have been terrified.

As I walked down the street, I attempted to puzzle out the identity of my abductors. All roads led to Robert Paris. They had been waiting for me when I came out of Grant's building. Whether Abrams had called them or they'd followed me into the city, it was clear that my nosing around had not gone unnoticed. Aaron had warned me I was being watched. Until this moment I hadn't believed him. The judge wanted to know how much I knew about Hugh's murder. Apparently, I didn't know enough to be gotten rid of. Yet.

Ahead of me I saw men walking up and down the street. I came to a corner and looked up. There was a red neon sign on an angle above a door. It said Febe's. I crossed the street and stood at the open doorway. Directly inside the entry was a brown vinyl curtain that reached to the floor, and beyond it I heard muffled noises. I pushed through the curtain just in time for last call at one of the most notorious leather bars in the city.

Two men were playing at a pinball machine on my left. One of them wore black leather pants, shiny in the dim light, and a leather vest. The other wore jeans, a t-shirt and a collar around his neck studded with metal spikes. He sipped from a bottle of Perrier. To my right there was a curved bar bathed in red lights. All heads turned toward me. In my slacks and gray polo shirt I was in the wrong clothes for Febe's. The atmosphere began to change from curiosity to hostility.

I had now been standing at the door for more than a minute. The bartender, undoubtedly thinking I was a tourist, scowled and started to come out from behind the bar. I took a couple of steps toward him and then passed out.

I was awakened with a hit of amyl nitrate.

"Jesus Christ," I muttered, pushing the donor's hands out of my face. "Enough."

The hands withdrew and a voice asked, "You all right?"

"I'm better," I said, sitting up from the floor.

The bartender knelt beside me. He was wearing a tight pair of levis and a pink bowling shirt with the name Norma Jean stitched above the pocket. Most of his face was lost behind a thick beard, but the concern in his wide blue eyes would have done justice to my mother.

"Good," he said. "I'll just call a cab and you can go back to the St. Francis or wherever you're staying and sleep it off."

"I'm not drunk," I said, slurring my words. "Drugged. I was drugged."

"Against your will?"

I nodded.

"Honey, that musta been some scene." He smiled. "He hurt you?"

I shook my head.

"Did he take your money?"

"No," I said, "they just drove me around and asked me questions."

"Now that's bizarre. Should I get the cops?"

"No, I'd like to call a friend."

"Oh, are you a local?"

I nodded.

"Hell, the way you came in here staring I thought you were a tourist who'd taken the wrong turn at Fisherman's Wharf."

"Next time," I mumbled, "I'll remember you have a dress code. Help me to the phone, okay?"

"Sure," he said, rising to his full height. I grabbed his extended hands and he raised me up, effortlessly. The bar was empty and all the lights were on, revealing a homey and rather shabby tavern. Apparently I'd cleared the place out. He led me around the bar to the house phone. "You make your call. I've got to clean up."

"Thanks. I know your name's not Norma Jean."

"Dean," he said, grabbing a broom.

"Thanks, Dean. I'm Henry." He nodded acknowledgement while I dialed Grant's number.

Grant picked up the phone on the second ring, and I remembered he was a light sleeper. I told him, briefly, what had learned and asked if he would come and pick me up. Wide awake, he told me to wait and that he was on his way. I hung up.

Dean brought me a glass of brandy and had me sit on a stool behind the bar as he went back to his work. I watched him lifting boxes of empty beer bottles and stacking them against the wall.

Someone was knocking at the front door. Dean glanced over at me and then went to answer it, behind the curtain. He emerged a second later followed by Grant Hancock. With his Burberry overcoat and perfectly groomed hair, Grant looked as if he had just stepped off the pages of a fashion magazine. Dean winked at me, approvingly.

Grant came up and inspected me. "You look terrible, Henry. Should we get you to a hospital?"

"I think everything's working," I said. "I just need a ride back to my car."

"Your car? What you need is sleep. Come on."

I got up and followed him out. Dean walked us to the curb where Grant had parked.

"Thanks, Dean." I reached out and patted his arm awkwardly, wanting to say more but not sure what.

"Come back sometime," he said, smiling. I climbed into Grant's car. We drove through the soundless streets to his building.

"I really should get back home tonight," I said.

"Henry, it's three-thirty in the morning," Grant replied as he steered into the underground garage and parked in a numbered stall. "No one has to do anything at three-thirty, especially you. You're hardly awake now. I doubt that you could make it all the way back."

"You're probably right," I said. "I'll stay."

"Of course you will," he replied, getting out of the car.

When we got to his condo, I took a hot shower, changed into borrowed clothes and asked for a drink. We sat on the floor in the living room drinking brandy by candlelight. The room was very still as Grant had me explain the events which occurred after I left his apartment.

"I think," he said, "that you are lucky to be alive."

"I agree, and now I know, beyond any doubt, that the judge was responsible for Hugh's death."

"So now you can stop and go on with your life."

"What?"

Grant swirled the brandy in his glass, watching it streak and run down the sides. "The mystery is solved."

"But I still have to prove the solution."

"To whom?"

"The police, to begin with, and maybe, at some point, a jury."

"Are you serious?" he asked, putting his glass down. "You think you can prove this against Robert Paris? Do you know anything about the man?"

"As a general proposition? No."

"You're talking about one of the most powerful men in the state," he said. "You're talking about a man who declined appointment to the United States Supreme Court."

"I didn't know that," I said.

"That's the point. Think of it this way, Henry. You and the judge both have piles of stones to throw at each other. You've pretty much used yours up but he hasn't even started. He's been playing with you."

"Schoolboys throw rocks at frogs in sport," I quoted, "but the frogs die in earnest."

"No," Grant said. "Not for sport. For power. I know Robert Paris," he continued, staring into his glass. "You don't stand a chance."

"Is this the voice of experience talking?"

Grant looked up. "My father," he began, "got it into his head that he wanted to be mayor of this city. Have you met my father?" I nodded. My recollection was of an elegant but rather dim patrician whom Grant inexplicably idolized. "Robert Paris was backing another candidate who would have trounced my father anyway. But just to make sure," he set his glass down and looked away, "they told my father I was gay and that if he persisted, the whole town would know. That's how my father found out his only son was homosexual. My father is a man," he continued, "who still thinks gay is a perfectly acceptable adjective for divorcees. Or did, anyway. It broke his heart," Grant said. "It really did."

"Grant, I'm sorry."

He shrugged. "That's water under the bridge," he said, "but the moral is: Don't fuck with Robert Paris. Hugh's dead. You're not." And then he added softly, "I'm not."

"But if it had been you rather than Hugh, I'd do the same."

He smiled a little. "You miss my meaning."

"No," I said, reaching out to touch his hand, "I don't."

□

"What time is it?" Grant mumbled, turning over in bed.

"A little after six," I replied, buttoning my shirt.

"You're leaving?"

"Yes, there's someone I have to see."

"Your associates keep odd hours." He sat up in bed, watching me tie my shoes.

"Will you call Smith for me?" I asked.

He thought about it a second.

"I still don't see the point of it," he said.

"The police wouldn't reopen their investigation without pressure from somewhere. Who better than Smith?"

"If you could only give me something more concrete," he said.

"If I didn't know you better, Grant, I'd say John Smith intimidates you."

"He does. It's not often I ask for an audience with a local deity."

"Okay," I said, "then don't."

"I'm sorry, Henry. I just can't see getting involved at this point."

"You've already been helpful, Grant."

"Thanks."

We looked at each other.

"Is this it, then?" he asked.

"No," I replied. "No."

I leaned over and kissed him.

"All right," he said.

□

An hour later I was finishing breakfast in Terry Ormes' kitchen. She cooked well for a cop, I thought as I swallowed a forkful of scrambled eggs. It occurred to me that I could not remember when I had eaten last. The eggs were good — she put tarragon in them. She was talking on the phone, explaining to someone why she would be late for work. I got up and cleared the table, rinsing dishes and stacking them in the dishwasher. Her kitchen was long, sunny and narrow. Everything was in its place but this bespoke an orderly presence rather than a fussy one. She finished her call and came back into the kitchen carrying a manila folder. She sat down at the kitchen table. I joined her there.

"More coffee?" she asked, pouring herself a cup.

"Sure," I said, noticing for the first time that the backs of her hands were covered with faint freckles.

"How long have you been a cop?" I asked, continuing our earlier conversation.

"Seven years, going on twenty."

"Tough life?"

"It's what I always wanted. My dad was a cop. He got as high up as captain before he retired."

"Did he want you to join the force?"

"He never came out and said it, but he was happy that I did."

"And your mother?"

"She'd have been happier if I'd gone into something more feminine. Schoolteaching, for instance, like my brother." She sipped her coffee. "What about you? Was your dad a lawyer?"

"No, he was foreman of the night crew at a cannery in Marysville. I'm the only lawyer in my family."

"The scuttlebutt around the station is that you're good."

"I am," I said.

"But you're not a great cop," she said, "judging from what happened to you last night. The first thing we learn is not to take unnecessary risks."

"And how do you know when a risk is unnecessary? I was playing a hunch going to see Abrams. I didn't think much would come from it. I was wrong."

"I'll say. Why don't you run your next scheme by me and let me decide if it's an unnecessary risk?"

I laughed. "Are you my partner or my mother?"

"I guess that depends on what you need most," Terry said. "Let's get to work."

She opened the manila folder and handed me a thin sheaf of papers.

"What's this?"

"Hugh Paris," she said. "Everything I could get on him."

"Doesn't seem like much."

"It isn't. He didn't have a California driver's license so I ran his name with DMV and came back with nothing. The only criminal record he has was his arrest in July. No credit cards, no known bank accounts. He leased his house from something called the Pegasus Corporation, one of those companies that owns companies."

I'd been going through the papers as I listened to her. "These are his phone bills?"

"For the last six months. Service was in his name. An unlisted number."

A fair number of the calls were to Portola Valley — the judge — and even a couple to my apartment. It was odd to see my phone number there and I wondered if anyone else had obtained these records. And then I noticed a number of calls made to Napa. I asked Terry about them.

"They were made to a private mental institution called Silverwood. You know anything about that?"

"His father is a patient there," I replied, writing the number down. I came to the last page. "I thought there'd be more."

"So did I. I get the feeling he was deliberately lying low." I nodded agreement. She took out a bundle of papers from the folder and pushed them across to me. "I had better luck with the grandmother and uncle," she said. I had asked her to find out what she could about the car crash which had killed Hugh's grandmother, Christina, and his uncle, Jeremy, twenty years earlier. Hugh had maintained that his grandfather was responsible for those deaths.

Terry had obtained copies of the accident report prepared by the CHP, written within a couple of hours of the collision. She had also gotten the coroner's findings based on an inquest held in San Francisco three days after the accident.

The CHP concluded that the car, driven by Jeremy Paris, had been headed east into Nevada on highway 80 at the time of the crash. It was dusk, a few days before Thanksgiving, the road was icy, traffic was light and there had been a snowstorm earlier in the week. The Paris car had been in the far left lane, nearest the center divider, a metal railing about four feet high. There was reason to believe that Jeremy Paris had been speeding.

About twenty miles outside of Truckee, disaster overcame the Parises. Their car suddenly went through the center divider, skidded off the side of the road across four lanes of westbound traffic, nearly hit a westbound car, and plunged off the road where its fall was broken by a stand of trees. Within a matter of moments, the car burst into flames. Christina Paris was dead when the police got to her, having been summoned by the driver of the car who had narrowly avoided being struck by the Paris car. Jeremy Paris died in the ambulance.

The driver of the other car, Warren Hansen, was the only witness and had provided details of the accident to the police. Hansen had been returning home to Sacramento from a week's skiing. He, the report noted in cop talk, was HBD — had been drinking, shorthand for drunk. Hansen claimed that the Paris car was going too fast for the road and that it appeared to be followed by another car, tailing it from the next lane over. He remembered that the second car was dark and its lights were off. He said that just before the accident the dark car had been striking against the back bumper of the Paris car.

All these statements were duly noted by the cop who took the report. They were then dismissed by the sergeant who signed off on the report and who remarked that Hansen was drunk and further disoriented by the shock of nearly having been in a serious collision. The sergeant concluded that Jeremy Paris had simply lost control of his car as he sped down the icy roads at dusk, the most treacherous hour for motorists. It was plausible. I could almost hear the sergeant sighing with relief as he filed the report; another mess averted.

I turned to the coroner's report. Sitting without a jury, he accepted the findings of the CHP as to the circumstances of the accident, based upon the brief testimony of a single witness, the sergeant. He added some information from the autopsies; charred meat is essentially all that had been left of Christina and Jeremy Paris. Finally, he fixed the times of their deaths. According to the coroner, given the circumstances of the accident and the conditions of the bodies, the deaths could be characterized as essentially simultaneous. When I came upon that phrase, simultaneous death, something clicked in the back of my mind.

I went on to the next page. It was a death certificate, made out for Warren Hansen who died on April 27, of a self-inflicted gunshot wound. Six months after the accident. I looked up at Terry.

"Up to this," I said, holding the death certificate, "I could almost believe it was just an accident."

"Me, too," she said. "But as soon as I got it, all the loose ends unraveled again." She explained that it made no sense to hold the inquest without calling the only eye-witness to the accident, or the paramedics who brought the bodies up from the crash and who could have testified to the times of death. "But then," she continued, "it dawned on me that that was the whole reason for the inquest. To set the times of death. There's no other reason to hold a coroner's inquest for a simple car accident. They don't usually call the coroner unless there's some question about the deaths."

"But there wasn't any question here," I said. "And certainly no reason to hold the inquest hundreds of miles from where the accident occurred and three days afterwards. The only difference between the police report and the coroner's inquest were the times of death. Someone wasn't happy with the fact that Jeremy Paris was still alive when they pulled him from the car."

"Naturally," she said, "I thought it was the judge who requested the coroner but I was wrong. It was John Smith, Christina's brother, who arranged it."

I thought for a moment. "Well, maybe he suspected," I replied, "and wanted a coroner's independent examination of the accident."

Terry laughed derisively.

"What?" I asked.

"That's not what Smith got," she said. "The examining coroner was Tom Fierro. Do you know about him?" I shook my head. "He's the guy they discovered with the suitcases of money under his bed. My dad used to talk about him and said that Tom was everyone's favorite coroner. When you bought him, he stayed bought."

"Do you think he was paid off?"

She sighed eloquently. "Of course I do, but who am I going to ask about it?" She gathered up the papers and stacked them neatly. "What's our next move?"

"All this means something," I mused, "and if I just sat still long enough it would come to me. But I can't sit still. These calls to Napa," I said, lifting the phone bills. "Maybe Hugh said something to his father that could help us. That's where I'm going. You work on finding out more about John Smith. He may hold the key."

"I don't know," she said, "I think there are too many doors for just one key. Stay in touch."

□

The street sign was so discreetly placed that I missed it the first time and drove on until I found myself at a dead end. I turned around and drove slowly until I saw that the narrow opening between clumps of dusty bushes was, in fact, a road; a back road off a back road at the edge of Napa's suburban sprawl.

It was one of those luminescent autumn days. The sky was radiantly blue and the air was warm and silty. You drank rather than breathed it. At my right, a white picket fence appeared and beyond it, orchards and pasture. These gave way to a large, formal lawn, arbors, tennis courts, and a rose garden, looking for all the world like the grounds of a country club.

Only there was no one around.

I looked over to my left and saw a white antebellum mansion shimmering like a mirage in the heat of the day. Smaller bungalows surrounded it at a respectful distance, each in the shade of its own great oak. One or two people moved slowly down a walk between the big house and one of the smaller ones. I turned into a circular driveway and drove up to a parking lot at the side of the house. I got out of my car and went up the steps of the great house, crossed the veranda and touched the doorbell.

Above the bell was a small brass plate with the word "Silver-wood" etched into it.

A husky young man dressed in orderly's white appeared at the door. "May I help you?"

"I've come to see Mr. Nicholas Paris," I said, extracting a business card from my breast pocket and handing it to him.

He studied it.

"Are you expected?"

"I was his late son's lawyer," I replied. "He'll know who I am."

The attendant looked at me and then opened the door. I stood in a massive foyer. There was a small table off the side of the staircase where he had been sitting. He went to the table, picked up the phone and dialed three numbers.

"There's a lawyer out here to see one of the patients." He paused. "Okay, clients, then. Anyway, he's out here now." He hung up and said, "Have a seat," gesturing me to a sofa against the wall beneath a portrait of a seventeenth-century gentleman. I sat down. The attendant went back to his book, something called The Other David. The house was still, but the air was nervous.

"Where are the patients?" I asked.

"Everyone takes a nap after lunch," he replied, looking up, "just like kindergarten."

"You a nurse?"

"Do I look like a nurse?" His muscles bulged against his white uniform. "I keep people out there," he gestured to the door, "from getting in and people in here from getting out."

"Nice work if you can get it," I observed.

He grunted and went back to his book.

A moment later, a short, bald man stepped into the foyer from a room off the side. He wore a white doctor's coat over a pale blue shirt and a red knit tie. He looked like an aging preppie and I was willing to bet that he wore argyle socks. The attendant handed him my business card.

"Mr. Rios," he said, "I'm Dr. Phillips, the director. Why don't we step into the visitor's lounge?"

I followed him into the room from which he had emerged. It was a long, narrow rectangle, paneled in dark wood, furnished in stiff-backed Victorian chairs and couches clustered in little groups around coffee tables. The view from the windows was of a rose garden. A dozen long-stemmed red roses had been stiffly arranged in a vase on the mantel of the fireplace. A grandfather clock ticked away in a corner. Except for us, the room was deserted.

Phillips lowered himself in a wing chair and I sat across from him. The little table between us held a decanter filled with syrupy brown fluid and surrounded by small wine glasses. He poured two drinks. I lifted a glass and sniffed, discreetly. Cream sherry. I sipped, crossing my legs at my ankles like a gentleman.

"Now, then, Mr. Rios, what can we," he said, using the imperial, medical we, "do for you?"

"I represent the estate of Hugh Paris, the son of one of your patients—"

"Clients," he cautioned.

"Clients," I agreed. "At any rate, Hugh Paris died rather — suddenly, and there are some problems with the will I believe I could clear up by speaking to his father, Nicholas."

Phillips shook his head. "That's quite impossible. You must know that Nicholas Paris is incompetent."

"Doctor, that's a legal conclusion, not a medical diagnosis. I was told he has moments of lucidity."

"Far and few between," Phillips said, dismissively. "Perhaps if you told me what you need, I could help you."

"All right," I said. "I drafted Hugh Paris's will which, as it happens, made certain bequests that violate the rule in Shelley's case, rendering the document ineffective. I had hoped that Mr. Paris, as his son's intestate heir, would agree to certain modifications that would effect the testater's intent, at least as to those bequests which do not directly concern his interests in the estate."

Phillips's eyes had glazed over at the first mention of the word will. He now bestirred himself and said, "I see."

"Then you understand my problem," I plunged on, "I am responsible for drafting errors in Hugh's will. There's some question of malpractice—"

Phillips perked up. "Malpractice?" He was now on comfortable ground. "I sympathize, of course, but Mr. Paris is hardly in any condition to discuss such intricate legal matters."

"I only need ten minutes with him," I said.

"Really," Phillips said, lighting a cigarette, "you don't understand. Mr. Paris is not lucid."

I could tell our interview was coming to an end.

I tried another tack. "But he's being treated."

Phillips lifted an eyebrow. "We can do very little of that in Mr. Paris's case. We try to make him comfortable and see that he poses no danger to himself or others."

"Is he violent?"

"Not very."

"Drugs?"

"The law permits it."

"You know, doctor," I said, "even those who cannot be reached by treatment can sometimes be reached by subpoena."

Phillips sat up. "What are you talking about?"

"A probate hearing, with all the trimmings. You might be called to testify to Paris's present mental condition and the type of care he's received here. It might even be necessary to subpoena his medical records. I understand he's been here for nearly twenty years. That's a long time, doctor, time enough to turn even a genius into a vegetable with the right kind of — treatment."

Phillips fought to keep his composure.

"I could have you thrown out," he said softly.

"And I'll be back with the marshal and a bushel of subpoenas."

In an even softer voice he asked, "What is it you want?"

"I want to make sure he's too crazy to sue me."

Phillips expelled his breath, disbelievingly. "Is that all?" He rose from the chair. "Ten minutes, Mr. Rios, and you'll go?"

"Never to darken your doorway again."

"Wait here," he said abruptly and left the room. I poured my sherry into a potted plant.

When Nicholas Paris entered the room, the air went dead around him. He wore an old gray blazer over a white shirt and tan khaki slacks. No belt. He might have been a country squire returning from a walk with his white-blond hair, ruddy complexion and composed features — there was more than a hint of Hugh in his face. But then you looked into his eyes. They were blue and they stared out as if from shadows focusing on a landscape that did not exist beneath the mild California sun. I felt the smile leak from my face. Phillips sat him down in a chair, scowled at me and said, "Ten minutes."

I approached him. "Nicholas?"

He inclined his head toward me.

"My name is Henry. I was Hugh's friend."

He said nothing.

I knelt beside the chair and looked at him. It was as if he were standing behind a screen: the thousand splinters refused to add up to a human face. I saw that his pupils were moving erratically. Drugs.

"I was his friend," I continued. "Your son Hugh."

He looked away, out the window.

He said in a voice hoarse from disuse, "Hugh."

"Hugh," I said.

I kept talking, softly. I told him how I had met Hugh and how much I had cared for him. I told him that I believed Hugh's death was a murder. I was telling him that I needed to know what, if anything, Hugh had said to him when he visited here.

Nicholas Paris stared out the window as I spoke, giving no indication that he heard anything but the loud chirping of a bird outside.

And then, suddenly, I saw a tear run from the corner of his eye. A single, streaky tear.

He said, "Is Hugh dead?"

He hadn't known.

"Oh, God," I muttered. "I'm sorry."

"That's enough," a woman spoke, commandingly, above me. I looked up. Katherine Paris stood, coldly composed, beside me. Her face was red beneath her makeup, and her small, elegant hands were clenched into fists. I glanced up at the doorway. Phillips was standing there and, behind him, two burly orderlies.

I rose from the floor. "Good afternoon, Mrs. Paris."

She raised a hand and slapped me. "Get him out of here," she ordered Phillips.

He gave a signal and the orderlies moved in.

— 7 —

It was dusk when Katherine Paris's bronze-colored Fiat came off the road that led from Silverwood and turned onto the highway. I switched off the radio, started my car, and followed her. There was no reason to think she would recognize my car; blue Accords are so common as to be almost invisible on the roads of California. She led me past vineyards, orchards, farm houses, and a desolate-looking housing tract with street names like Chardonnay and Pinot Noir. It was getting chilly out, a sign of autumn in the air. We drove on and on, deeper into the country between gently wooded hills now gloomy in the thick blue light of early evening. She turned her lights on and I turned on mine. A truck roared by and then a motorcycle and then it was just the two of us again, and the dense smell of wet earth rising from the darkened fields around us.

It would have been nice, I thought, had Hugh Paris been beside me. There was a restaurant in St. Helena that I'd been to once and liked. We could have driven there for dinner and stayed overnight somewhere and visited the wineries the next day. Eliot had it wrong about memory and desire; they smelled like wet earth on an autumn night and had nothing to do with spring.

My thoughts drifted back to the task at hand. The Fiat's turn signal flashed on and we went down a narrow road. A brightly-lit three-story building rose just ahead of us. A sign above the entrance identified it as the Hotel George. The hotel was constructed of wood, painted white with green trim, a charming old place. A wide porch surrounded the first floor and chairs were lined up near the railing. They were mostly empty now. She parked and I watched her climb the steps and walk quickly across the porch into the building.

I waited in my car to see whether she would come out. There were some hot springs in the vicinity and I imagined that the George was a place from which people commuted to them. There were only three other cars in the lot; business, apparently, was slow.

When she failed to come out after five minutes, it occurred to me that Mrs. Paris might be meeting someone. Who? A member of the family? It was a small family to begin with and events had savaged it.

Of Linden's grandchildren, John and Christina Smith, only Christina married. She and Robert had two sons, Jeremy and Nicholas. Of the two sons only Nicholas married and he and Katherine had produced only one child, Hugh. Of these four generations, the only survivors were John Smith, the judge, mad Nicholas and Katherine herself. The decimation of Grover Linden's descendents proceeded as if in retribution. I shook myself out of my musing and realized that another five minutes had passed. I decided to go in after her.

The lobby was a little rectangular space, the floor covered with a thick gray carpet, the furnishings dark Spanish-style chairs and tables. A polished staircase beside the registration desk led to the upper floors. Across from the desk was an open door with a small neon sign above the doorway identifying it as the bar. I went over and looked in. Through the dimly-lit darkness I could see her, sitting on a high stool at the end of the bar. I walked in and approached her from behind. She was alone.

I took the stool next to her, ordering bourbon and water. I wished her a good evening.

Her head swiveled toward me until we were face to face. I saw exhaustion in her eyes so deep that it quickly extinguished the flash of anger that registered when she recognized me. There was contempt in her look and disdain and beneath it all a plea to be left alone. I regretted that I could not comply.

"May I buy you a drink, Mrs. Paris?"

"Why not," she said mockingly. "I'm sure they'll take your money here and I never refuse a drink." I summoned the bartender and ordered refills. "You follow me here?"

"Yes."

"Why?"

"To talk."

"About Hugh?"

"Not necessarily. We could talk about you. Or your husband. Or your ex-father-in-law."

"I find none of those subjects appealing," she said. The darkness of the room cast shadows that hid all but the deepest lines in her face and she looked like a much younger woman. She was small, her feet not reaching to the metal ring at the bottom of the barstool, and, for an instant, as she lifted her drink she looked as fragile as a child.

"Then tell me about your poetry."

She looked sidewise at me. "Mr. Rios, I once had a talent for writing, a very small talent. I used it up a long time ago, or drank it up, perhaps. At any rate, that subject is the least appealing of all." After a moment's silence, she asked abruptly, "Do you like your life?"

"You mean, am I happy?"

'Yes, if you want to be vulgar about it." She finished her drink. Another soldier down.

"I have been, from time to time."

"A lawyer's answer," she said disdainfully. "Mincing — oh, pardon me. Equivocal. What I mean is," and her voice was suddenly louder, "on the whole, wouldn't you rather be dead?"

"No."

"Well I often think I would," she said softly.

"Why?"

She shook her head. "Every drop of meaning has been squeezed from my life. I hardly expect you to understand."

"Your husband?"

"My husband," she said. Another drink had appeared in front of her. I realized that I was about to be the recipient of the drunken confidences of an old, depressed woman. Common decency almost got me out of the bar, but not quite. "I married

Nick Paris in my sophomore year at Radcliffe. I had an old Boston name and no money. He was rich and crazy. I knew about the rich but not the crazy." She scraped a fingernail across the surface of her glass. "I wanted to be Edna St. Vincent Millay, Mr. Rios. Instead, I became a crazy rich man's wife. And a minor poet." She stared at me as if trying to remember who I was. "What is it you want from me?"

"Who killed Hugh?"

"Oh, that. Why do you think anyone killed Hugh. He was quite capable of killing himself."

"And you would rather be dead but here you are, alive and well."

"Alive, perhaps. I can't help you, darling. I was bought and paid for long ago."

"By whom?"

"Surely you know enough about this family to know by whom. When I married Nick his parents were horrified by my poverty, tried to buy an annulment but by then I was pregnant with Hugh. We came out to California and things were fine for awhile. Christina, my mother-in-law, treated me quite well. And Jeremy, of course, I was quite fond of."

"Your brother-in-law."

She nodded. "Then it went bad." She lit a cigarette.

"What happened?"

"Christina wanted a divorce. Her husband wouldn't hear of it."

"The judge."

"Of course. The marriage was working for him. He had what he wanted from the family — money, power, prestige. And he treated her like a chattel and his sons like less than that. He is, you know, a malevolent human being."

"I gathered."

She looked at me. "Hugh tell you some stories? I assure you, there are worse." She expelled a stream of cigarette smoke toward her reflection in the barroom mirror. "Then they were killed, Christina and Jeremy."

"Do you know where they were going at the time?"

"To Reno. Christina was to obtain a divorce. Jerry went for

moral support. It was all very conspiratorial. They left early in the morning without telling the judge, but he found out. The next day they brought the bodies back."

"He killed them."

"Do your own addition," she said. "Nicholas was already sick by then. He really loved Jeremy and after Jeremy's death he deteriorated pretty quickly. Perhaps not so quickly as to warrant that lunatic bin, but that's a matter for the doctors to dispute."

"And what happened to you?"

"I was having an affair at the time," she said, "and Paris — the judge — hired an investigator to document my indiscretion. He demanded that I agree to a divorce and renounce my rights to Nick's estate. Unfortunately, I had acquired a taste for wealth, so I was desperate to salvage something. And, as it happened, I had a pawn to play." She touched a loose strand of hair, tucking it back.

"Hugh?"

"Yes. His father's heir. I gave Paris custody of my son and got in exchange—"

"Your thirty pieces of silver," I said bitterly.

"Considerably more than that," she said. "And what right do you have to judge me? He was nothing to you but a trick."

"No," I said. "I loved him."

She looked away from me. A moment later she said, "I have never understood homosexuality. I can't picture what you men do with each other."

"I could tell you but it would completely miss the point."

"I'm sorry, Mr. Rios, and about so many things it's hardly worth while to begin enumerating them now."

"Would you like me to drive you back into the city?"

"No, thank you. The bartender cuts me off at ten and I take a room in the hotel. I'll be fine." She had stepped down from the barstool. "Goodnight, Mr. Rios."

"Goodnight, Mrs. Paris."

Then she was gone, weaving between tables toward a door marked Ladies. I went out into the darkness and the chilly autumn air, drunk and depressed.

□

The next morning I was at the county law library when it opened and spent the next hour ploughing through treatises on the law of trusts and estates. The coroner's phrase, that Christina and Jeremy Paris had died simultaneously, had been ticking away in the back of my mind. I'd thought about it all the way back from Napa. There had to be a reason for the discrepancy between the times of death recorded at the scene of the accident and the coroner's finding. The coroner's report was a legal document and there were only two areas of the law to which it pertained, criminal and probate. Since, at the time, there was no issue of criminal liability arising from the accident, the coroner's findings must have been sought for the purposes of the probate court. When I got to that point, I remembered simultaneous death, a phrase I recollected dimly from my trusts and estates class.

I picked up a red-covered casebook, *Testate and Intestate Succession*, eighth edition, by John Henry Howard, Professor Emeritus at Linden University School of Law. Professor Howard had been my teacher for trusts and estates. Back then, he was only up to his fifth edition. I opened the book to the general table of contents. The book was divided into the two main sections, intestate and testate succession. Seeing the two concepts juxtaposed in type on facing pages, I suddenly realized my research mistake. Aaron Gold had told me that Christina Paris had left a will but her estate, nonetheless, passed through intestacy. I had focused on whether there could be a drafting error that would invalidate a will and which, somehow, involved times of death. But the rule of simultaneous death was a concept of intestate succession and it functioned whether a will was properly drawn or not; the issue was not whether a will was correctly drafted, but who it named as a beneficiary. I turned to the more detailed table of contents and, under intestate succession, buried near the bottom of the page, saw the words simultaneous death.

It was not a not a hot topic in the law of estates, rating little more than a page and a half. One page was a general discussion of the concept, with case citations. The other half-page presented a hypothetical situation and a number of questions arising from it. I remembered that Professor Howard's hypos were never as easy as they first looked.

Given the byzantine complications of most estate law, the concept of simultaneous death was relatively simple and straightforward. The underlying premise was that neither a dead person nor his estate should be permitted to inherit a bequest by one living. Consequently, if a woman left her estate to her daughter but her daughter predeceased her, the gift was void. Upon the mother's death the gift reverted to her estate rather than passing to the daughter's heirs.

But what happened if mother and daughter died in such a manner that it was impossible to tell who died first? Did the gift revert to the mother's estate or pass to the daughter's? It was for such a contingency that the rule of simultaneous death arose. Using this rule, the law presumed that where the testator and beneficiary died simultaneously, the beneficiary died first. Consequently, the gift reverted to the estate of the giver and was distributed according to the rest of her testamentary scheme.

So it made no difference whether the will was properly written or not. For instance, a father might make a will leaving everything he owned to his son, but if the son died before the father the will became just a scrap of paper and the father's estate was divided as if the will had never existed. I was beginning to think that something very similar to that had occurred in the case of Christina Paris.

There was one other point about the rule of simultaneous death that had special meaning for me. The presumption, that the testator survived the beneficiary, was rebuttable. This meant that it could be disputed in court by competent evidence. The testimony, say, of the paramedics at the scene of the accident. But if all the probate court had before it was the coroner's report, it was not likely to look further; a court may believe or disbelieve the evidence submitted to it, but it has no means by which to conduct its own investigations.

I turned to the hypothetical. At first glance the facts seemed simple enough, but I read the hypo more carefully the second time looking for land mines. Halfway through it occurred to me that the facts were suspiciously familiar: a wealthy woman left her entire estate to one of her two sons who, subsequently, was killed in the same car accident that killed her. Was it possible that Professor Howard had based this hypo on the facts of Christina Paris's death? Beneath the hypo, Professor Howard provided six additional facts, each of which changed the disposition of the woman's estate. Number six asked whether it would make any difference to the distribution of her wealth if one of her intestate heirs — her husband, perhaps — had arranged the deaths precisely to invalidate the will. *Her husband, perhaps?*

□

Two hours later I was walking alongside a dusty hedge on a dead-end street in an obscure wooded pocket of the campus where retired professors lived in university-subsidized houses. While it was generally acknowledged at the law school that John Howard, who'd retired eight years earlier, was still alive, he was seldom seen and even more rarely contacted. Finally, some antiquarian in the alumni office had found an address for me.

I came to a white picket gate. Across a weedy, dying lawn and in the shade of an immense oak tree stood a stucco house. It was remarkably still and peaceful-looking, like a ship harbored in calm waters. I pushed the gate open and went up the flagstones to a green door. There was a brass knocker in the shape of a gavel. I knocked, twice.

The door was opened by a middle-aged Asian woman wearing a green frock. She wiped her hands on her apron and eyed me suspiciously. "Yes?"

"I've come to see Professor Howard. Are you Mrs. Howard?"

"Housekeeper," she replied. "You want professor?"

"Yes, does he live here?"

"Sure," she said, "but long time no one comes."

"Well, I'm here," I pointed out.

"I'll get," she said, hurrying away. She'd left the door open so I stepped inside.

There was an odd smell in the house, musty and faintly sweet, a mixture of cigar smoke and furniture polish. I was standing at the end of a long dark hall. An arched entrance led off to a little living room. The furniture, old and very ugly, was too big for the room, as if purchased for some other house of grander proportions. A vacuum cleaner had been parked between two brick-red sofas. There were ashes of a fire in the fireplace. A pot of yellow chrysanthemums blazed on a coffee-table near a tidy stack of legal periodicals. The walls exuded an elderly loneliness. He probably never married, I thought.

The housekeeper appeared, touched my arm and told me to come with her. I followed down the hall and into a bright little kitchen. She opened the door to the back yard and I stepped outside. I saw an empty ruined swimming pool, the bottom filled with yellow leaves. Facing the pool were two white lawn chairs — the old-fashioned wooden ones — and between them a matching table. There was a fifth of vodka, a pint of orange juice and two glasses on the table. One of the chairs was occupied by an old man wearing a sagging red cardigan frayed through at the elbow.

He turned his face to me. His thick gray hair was greasy and disheveled. He now sported a wispy goatee. He held a cigar in one hand as he reached for a glass with his other. Professor John Henry Howard, latest edition.

"You wanted to see me?" he asked in a voice thickened with the sediment of alcohol and old age.

I nodded.

"Well, boy, introduce yourself."

"Henry Rios, sir. Class of '72. I took trusts and estates from you."

He peered at me intently as I approached, hand outstretched. He put down the cigar, shook my hand and motioned me to sit beside him. "'72? A good class, that. Not that many of you cared for probate. No, you belonged more to the quick than the dead. Where did you sit, Mr. —"

"Rios. In the back row."

"Ah, one of those. What was your final grade?"

"An A-minus."

He lifted his shaggy eyebrows and for a second I thought he was going to demand to see my transcript.

"Well, you must've learned something. Have a drink."

"No, I—," but before I could finish he'd filled the glass with vodka and added, as an afterthought, a splash of orange juice. I sipped. It was like drinking rubbing alcohol.

"The smart cocktail," the professor said touching his glass to mine. "One of my remaining pleasures. I have a system, you see. I allow myself only as much vodka as I have orange juice. Through judicious pouring I can make a pint of orange juice last all day."

"The legal mind at work," I said.

Professor Howard chuckled. "Indeed. So, Mr. Rios, what are we going to talk about?"

"I want to ask you about a hypo that appears in your casebook."

"You a probate lawyer?"

"No."

"Good, because if you were I'd charge you, and I ain't cheap. Proceed." He tilted his head back.

I withdrew from my pocket a xeroxed copy of the page in his book with the illustration of simultaneous death. "It's this," I said, handing it to him.

"What's the question?" he asked as he skimmed the page.

"A wealthy woman and her oldest son are killed in an auto accident. She'd devised her entire estate to that son. The court uses the rule of simultaneous death to invalidate the will and her estate passes, through intestacy, to her husband. Now here, in number six, you ask what effect it would have on the distribution of the estate if her husband had actually arranged the accident."

"Well, think, Mr. Rios," he prodded. "If you killed your old mother to obtain the family jewels, do you think the court would reward your matricide?"

"I take it from your tone the answer is no."

"If the law was otherwise it would be open season on every person of means. That answer your question?"

"One of them. These facts are based on the deaths of Christina and Jeremy Paris, aren't they?"

He picked up his cigar from the edge of the table and lit it.

"I'm investigating the death of her grandson, Hugh Paris, who was a friend of mine. I believe he knew or suspected that her death and the death of her son, Jeremy, was arranged by Robert Paris. I think you know something about that."

"What kind of law did you say you practice?"

"I didn't. Criminal defense."

He shook his head. "Criminal is a troublesome area. No rules. Might makes right, with only the thin paper of the Constitution between the fist and the face."

"Why did he have them killed?"

Howard regarded me through narrowed eyes, as if deciding whether or not to lie.

"She was on her way to obtain a divorce. That would've extinguished his intestate rights. She'd already cut him out of her will."

"How do you know that?"

"I drafted the will," he said, tremulously.

"What else do you know, professor?"

"About the will or the marriage? They were intertwined. The marriage was hell for her but she put up with it for the children and because she was Catholic and, not least of all, because she was Grover Linden's granddaughter and the Lindens don't acknowledge defeat. But she hated Robert. He used her, robbed her. So she came to me one night and told me to write her a will that would cut him off from the Linden money in such a way that he would lose if he contested it."

"How did you do it?"

"We gave him all the community property, his and hers. It was not an insignificant amount. That was the carrot. Everything else went to their sons. Jeremy was given his share outright and Nicholas's was put in a trust to be administered by Jeremy and his uncle, John Smith. That was the stick."

"I don't see it."

"Robert could hardly complain he wasn't provided for since he got everything they'd accumulated in thirty years of marriage. And should he contest the will that would put him in the position of challenging the rights of his own sons as well as his brother-in-law, a man richer even than he. For good measure, we threw in an in terrorem clause providing that he would lose everything if he unsuccessfully challenged any clause of the will."

"You thought of everything," I said, admiringly.

"Except one thing. His intestate rights. As long as they remained married, he was her principal intestate heir. So, from his perspective it was just a question of invalidating the will."

"Did he know about it, then?"

"Yes. She made the mistake of taunting him with it. Two weeks later she and Jeremy, who had dined together at her home, became seriously ill with food poisoning. It may have been a fluke that Robert, who ate the same things, was unaffected." The professor shrugged. "It frightened her. By then I had discovered the hole in our scheme. I advised her to get a divorce."

"She never made it," I said.

He breathed noisily and sucked at his now unlit cigar.

"I have only one other question. Why did she come to you?"

"Mr. Rios," he said, "that's ancient history."

"Please?"

"Almost sixty years ago," he said, "I attended a reception at this university given by Jeremiah Smith who was then in the thirtieth year of his presidency. His wife was dead and so his daughter, Christina, functioned as his hostess. I was nine months out of law school, just hired as a part-time lecturer in property law. Robert Paris was also at the reception, my colleague at the law school with about three months more experience than I. Well, Robert and I dared each other to approach the grand Miss Smith and ask her to dance. I did, finally. I got the dance, but he got the marriage, four years later. She and I became friends, though. We were always friends."

"I'm sorry."

He smiled, crookedly and without humor. "You know, Mr. Rios, there is one aspect of this case which you have failed to examine adequately."

"Sir?"

"Jeremy's death. Why was it necessary to kill the two of them in such a manner that simultaneous death could be found? Robert, as Jeremy's father, was Jeremy's principal intestate heir, since Jeremy had neither wife nor children. He could've picked Jeremy off at his leisure unless what?"

"Unless Jeremy had also executed a will that named a beneficiary other than the judge."

"Precisely."

"And did he?"

"Yes. It was still in draft form but it would've sufficed."

"Who was Jeremy's beneficiary?"

"His nephew, Hugh Paris."

"What became of Jeremy's will?

"I have it, somewhere. I brought it out only six months ago to show Hugh."

"Hugh was here?"

"Yes. He came to me knowing less than you do but enough to have guessed the significance of the fact that his uncle and grandmother were killed at the same time."

"They weren't, you know," I said. "She died before him by fifteen minutes. That's what the police report said, but the coroner was bribed to find otherwise."

He closed his eyes. "If I had known that twenty years ago, I would've gone to the police. How could Robert have been so clumsy?"

"I think he was desperate," I said. "Unnerved. If he'd been accused then, he might have fallen apart."

"And your friend would be alive," he said. "Now, I'm sorry."

And after that, there didn't seem to be anything left to say.

□

I left the professor and walked back to the student union where I found a phone and called Terry Ormes at the police station. She was out in the field so I left a message. Sonny Patterson at the D.A.'s office was out to lunch. I set up an appointment to see him the next morning. No one was answering at Aaron Gold's office. I hung up the phone feeling cheated, like an actor robbed of his audience. I stood indecisively in front of the phone booth until the smells from the cafeteria behind me reminded me it was time to eat.

I bought two hamburgers and two plastic cups of beer and took them to a corner table. As I ate, I put the case together the way I would present it to Sonny the next day.

It was a simple tale of greed. Robert Paris had been disinherited by his wife, Christina, in favor of his two sons, Nicholas and Jeremy. Nicholas posed no problems. He was mentally ill and could be easily controlled by the judge. Jeremy, however, had to be gotten rid of. Paris had to invalidate Christina's will in such a way as to strike her bequest to Jeremy, and any of his heirs, so that he himself might inherit that portion of Christina's estate through intestacy. Christina and Jeremy were killed in an accident to which there was but one witness who himself was later killed. A crooked coroner presided at the inquest and manipulated the times of death, making it appear that Christina and Jeremy died simultaneously. By operation of the rule of simultaneous death, Christina's estate passed to her remaining family, half to the judge through intestacy and half to his younger son, Nicholas, by operation of Christina's bequest which was not affected by the invalidity of the bequest to Jeremy.

Nicholas was then committed to an asylum and his wife, Katherine, blackmailed into a divorce. I had no doubt that the judge had been appointed conservator of Nicholas's estate. By the time the wheels of his machinations came to a stop, Judge Paris had secured control of his wife's fortune.

There was only the smallest of hitches: Hugh. In Hugh's case the judge acted more subtly. He took the boy from his mother, sexually abused him, and then set him adrift in a series of private schools far from his home. The judge made sure that Hugh had all the money he could spend. Rootless, without direction, with too much money and not enough judgment, Hugh became a wastrel, a hype. He very nearly self-destructed. But not quite. He came home, pieced together the story of his grandfather's crimes and suddenly became a serious threat to Robert Paris. So he too was killed.

That was the story. The evidence would not be as seamless or easily put together. It would come in bits and pieces, fragments of distant conversations, scribbled notes, fading memories. The investigation would be laborious and involve, undoubtedly, protracted legal warfare. Sonny might look at it, see the potential quagmire and look the other way. But I doubted it. I knew, from trying cases against him, that he didn't run from a fight. And he liked to win.

At least my part would be over. I would finally be able to exorcise that last image of Hugh lying in the morgue.

I got up and went back to the phone. This time Terry was in her office.

"Listen, I'm glad you called back," she began.

"I'm seeing Patterson in the morning. I'm going to lay out the whole story for him and I'd like you to be there."

"What story is that?"

"Robert Paris killed his wife, his son and his grandson. I know exactly how it happened and why. I'm sure Patterson will order the investigation into Hugh's death reopened."

"I don't think so," Terry said softly. "Where are you?"

"At the university. The student union. Why?"

"Have you seen this morning's paper?"

"No, not yet. I've been on the move since I got up."

"You better take a look at it."

"Why?"

"Robert Paris is dead. The judge is dead."

"What?"

"Early this morning. A stroke. Henry? You still there?"

"Yeah," I mumbled, looking across the patio of the student union to the courtyard. There were three flag poles there, one for a flag of the United States, one for a flag of California and the third for the university's flag. Having spent most of the day on campus I'd passed those poles maybe four or five times not noticing until this moment that the three flags flew at half-mast.

– 8 –

There was a burst of organ music as the doors to the chapel opened and the archbishop of San Francisco, flanked by red-skirted altar boys, stepped blinking into the bright light of midday. The university security guards who had been lounging in the vicinity of the doors now closed ranks, forming a loose cordon on either side of the funeral procession.

I was standing against a pillar next to a camera crew from a local T.V. station. A blond woman spoke softly into a microphone. The television lights exploded at the appearance of the first dignitaries emerging from the darkness of the church.

The mayor of San Francisco, an alumna, came out on the arm of the president of the university. Following a step or two behind came the governor, a graduate of the law school, walking alone, working the crowd with discreet waves and a slack smile. Next came a coterie of old men who, even without their robes, had the unmistakable, self-important gait of judges. For a moment afterward the threshold was empty. Then came eight elderly men dressed in similar dark suits, white shirts and black ties, shouldering the gleaming rosewood coffin.

Inside that box were the mortal remains of Robert Wharton Paris, who had been eulogized that morning by the San Francisco Chronicle as one of the most distinguished Californians of his time. No mention was made that the judge's sole surviving descendant, his son, was locked up in an asylum in Napa. Instead, the newspapers looked back on what was, inarguably, a dazzlingly successful life.

Robert Paris, who was born into a poor family of farmers in

the San Joaquin valley eighty years earlier, worked his way through Linden University, went to Oxford as a Rhodes scholar, and returned to the United States to take a law degree from Harvard, all before his twenty-fifth birthday. Hired as an instructor in property law at the university law school he quickly rose to the rank of full professor. In the process, he married Christina Smith, the granddaughter of Grover Linden and daughter of Jeremiah Smith, the university's first president.

Paris left the law school to form, with two of his colleagues, a law firm in San Francisco that now occupied its own building in the heart of the financial district. He resigned from the firm to accept appointment to the United States Court of Appeals for the Ninth Circuit. He was a distinguished jurist frequently mentioned as a potential candidate for the U.S. Supreme Court but he was too conservative for the liberal Democrats who then occupied the White House. When he was finally offered a position on the Court by a Republican president, he was forced to decline, citing age and physical infirmity. Shortly afterwards he left the court of appeals and spent the last decade of his life in virtual seclusion. Now, he was dead.

Greater than the man was what he represented, the Linden fortune. The media estimated the extent of that fortune at between five-hundred million and one billion dollars, but so cloaked in secrecy were its sources and tributaries that no one really knew. There was so much money that it had acquired an air of fable as though it were stored not in banks, trust companies and investment management firms, but hidden away in caves as if it were pirate treasure.

Famous money. Money gouged out of the Sierra Nevadas by the tens of thousands of picks that laid out the route of the transcontinental railroad. Ruthless money. Money acquired at the expense of thousands of small farmers forced from their farms by the insatiable appetite of Grover Linden's land companies.

Corrupt money. Money paid in subsidies to Grover Linden's railroad from the Congress in an era when the prevailing definition of an honest politician was one who, when bought, stayed bought.

Endless money. Money flowing so ceaselessly that during a

financial crisis in the 1890's, Grover Linden essentially guaranteed the national debt out of his own fortune and the government averted bankruptcy.

Robert Paris was steward to that fortune and only I, and perhaps one or two others, knew at what cost he had acquired his stewardship. I watched them carry him across the courtyard, and I was thinking not of the family of a nineteenth-century American railroad baron but of the Caesers, the Borgias, the Romanovs. Only on that dynastic scale could I begin to comprehend how a man might kill his wife, his child, his grandchild to satisfy an appetite for power.

I remembered a painting by Goya that I'd seen, years earlier, in the Prado called *Saturn Devouring His Children*. Saturn consumed his sons and daughters to avoid the prophecy that one son would reach manhood and depose his father. The mother of Zeus substituted for the infant Zeus a stone wrapped in swaddling clothes, which Saturn ate. Hidden away, Zeus grew and ultimately fulfilled the prophecy. Had Robert Paris feared the same end from his male descendants? Or was he simply mad? Or had that family of farmers in San Joaquin been poorer than anyone could imagine?

Meanwhile, the funeral had become a party for the rich. The crowd spilled out from the church, sweeping across the courtyard of the Old Quad to the driveway where I had earlier observed a fleet of limosines lined up behind a silver hearse. So loud and jovial were the mourners that I expected, at any moment, to be offered a cocktail or a canapé from a roving waiter. There were no signs of real grief; only, now and then, a ceremonial tear dabbed at with an elegant, monogrammed handkerchief. The rich are different, I thought: condemned to live their lives in public, they go through their paces at the edge of hysteria like show dogs from which every trait has been bred but anxiety. The body was to be interred in the Linden mausoleum, a quarter-mile distant. Judging from the snarl of cars in the driveway, I'd be able to walk there before the internment began.

The heat was slow and intense, a pounding, relentless, unseasonable heat. I set off down the road sweating beneath my fine clothes like any animal. In a way it was pointless for me to have come to the funeral. Lord knows there was nothing more to be done about Robert Paris except, perhaps, drive a stake through his heart.

I beat everyone to the mausoleum but the press. This was a historic event. No one had been laid to rest in Grover Linden's tomb since the death of his son-in-law, Jeremiah Smith, first president of the university, fifty years earlier. The lesser members of the Linden-Smith-Paris clan, including the judge's wife and eldest son, were buried in a small graveyard two hundred feet away. Hugh, however, was not there. I had never learned what became of his ashes.

I removed my jacket, positioned myself in the shade of an oak tree and studied Grover Linden's resting place. The legend was that Linden wanted his tomb patterned after the temple of the Acropolis. What he got was a much smaller building constructed from massive blocks of polished gray granite adorned on three sides with Ionic columns. At the entrance there were two steps which led to a bronze screen and beneath it two stone doors. On each side, the entrance was flanked by a marble sphinx.

In front of the tomb was an oval of grass bounded by a circular pathway, a tributary of the footpaths that criscrossed the surrounding wood. That wood was a popular trysting place, and it was not unusual to find the grounds near the tomb littered with beer cans, wine bottles, marijuana roaches, and used condoms. Today, however, the groundskeepers had been thorough.

I heard cars pulling up and then the cracking of wood as people surged forward from the road trampling the dry grass and fallen twigs; the more-or-less orderly procession across the Old Quad had become a curiosity-seeking mob, red-faced and sweaty, converging from all directions as the university security guards fought to keep open a corridor from the road to the steps of the tomb. I watched a photographer shimmy up one of the venerable oaks and stake out her position among its branches.

Finally the pallbearers appeared, walking slowly and stumblingly across the uneven dirt path. They were preceded by the school's president, who climbed the steps of the tomb and opened the doors. As he fiddled with the locks, one of the pallbearers, an old man, started to sink beneath the weight of his burden. Two security guards hurried to his side and propped him up. His mouth hung open and a vein beat furiously at his temple.

"Welcome to necropolis," a voice beside me murmured. I turned to find Grant Hancock standing beside me, cool and handsome in a light gray suit. "Do you see that gentleman there?"

I followed his gaze to a shadowy corner at the far edge of the crowd from where a tall thin old man surveyed the chaos from behind a pair of dark glasses.

"John Smith," I said. "I hadn't noticed him at the church."

"He wasn't in attendance," Grant said. The old man slipped away. "One titan buries another," Grant remarked.

"Cut from the same cloth?"

"God, no," Grant said. "Robert Paris was so vulgar he had buildings named in his honor while he was still alive. The only thing for which Smith has permitted use of his name is a rose."

"A rose?"

"He's an amateur horticulturist," Grant said. "Incidentally, what are you doing here?"

"I wanted to make sure he was dead."

He picked a fragment of bark from my shoulder and said, "It was open casket. He's dead."

"Open casket? That was vulgar."

"Robert Paris never did anything tastefully except die in his sleep. As for me, when I die I'll direct my family to bury me without fanfare."

I smiled. "When you die, Grant, the tailors and barbers will declare a day of national mourning."

"And when you die," he said, not quite as lightly, "I'll miss you." We began walking. "In fact, I've missed you the past four years."

I said nothing, feeling the sun on my neck, thinking of the funeral, thinking of Hugh, thinking as usual of too many things.

Grant said, "I've changed."

"Only very young people believe that change is always for the better," I said. "I'm mostly interested in holding the line, which is, I guess, the difference between thirty and thirty-four."

"Am I being rejected? Again?"

"No."

We had reached his car. He leaned against it and we looked at each other.

"I feel very old today," I said, "as though I've dissipated my promise and my capacity to love. I've felt that way since Hugh died. I don't know what there is left of me to offer."

"Let me decide that."

I nodded. "I'll drive up this weekend."

"Good, I'll see you then."

I walked back to my car and got in. I loosened my tie and rolled up my sleeves, tossing my jacket into the back seat. On the front seat was a book I'd bought that morning, *The Poems of C.P. Cavafy*, the poet Hugh had mentioned to me that distant summer evening in San Francisco. I glanced at my watch. It was almost one, time to drive to the restaurant where I was meeting Terry Ormes for lunch. I picked up the book. Flipping through it at the bookstore I'd marked a page with the little poem that I now read aloud:

The surroundings of the house, centers, neighborhoods
which I see and where I walk; for years and years.
I have created you in joy and in sorrows:
out of so many circumstances, out of so many things.
You have become all feeling for me.

The words had a liturgical cadence, almost a prayer. You have become all feeling for me. I had not come to see Robert Paris buried, but to bury Hugh. And still I was dissatisfied. I put the book down and started up the car.

□

Terry ran her fingertip around the rim of her glass of wine as I ordered another bourbon and water. The lunchtime crowd at Barney's had thinned considerably since we'd been seated an hour earlier. The plate of pasta in front of me was mostly uneaten, but I'd refused the waiter's attempts to clear it away. The presence of food helped me justify the amount of bourbon I was drinking.

Terry wore a satiny cotton dress, white with thin red and blue vertical stripes. A diamond pendant hung from her slim neck. Looking at her I wondered if she had a lover. I didn't imagine many men could accept her calm self-possession and luminous intelligence without feeling threatened. And, just now, she also looked beautiful to me.

"I should be getting back to work," she said, making no effort to move. Instead she poured the last of the wine from the bottle into her glass. Continuing our conversation, she asked, "What is it you can't accept?"

I shrugged. "Robert Paris's death, I guess. I wanted a confrontation and he ups and dies on me."

"But you don't think he was killed?"

"No. Apparently he's been in bad health for years and he died of natural causes."

"Then let it rest," she said. She sipped her wine. "What are you going to do with yourself now?"

"I don't know. I'm completely unprepared for anything other than the practice of law."

"That sounds like a good reason to do something else."

"I agree, but the details of my new life are — elusive."

The waiter deposited my drink in front of me and made another play for my plate. This time I let him take it.

"Just watch the whiskey intake," she said.

"I have to get my calories somewhere."

"You might come to my house for dinner some night."

"I'd like that."

We looked at each other.

"I'm offering as a friend," she said.

"I know. I accept."

I saw her look away. What did she see when she looked at me, I wondered. An alien or just a lonely man? The latter, I thought. Her dinner invitation came out of compassion, not curiosity.

"We're both different, Terry. We play against expectation and we're good at what we do. It's our competence that makes us outsiders, not the fact that you're a woman cop or I'm a gay lawyer."

She nodded, slightly, and made a movement to leave. I rose with her.

"Take care of yourself, Henry. Go away for a few days, meet someone new, and when you get back, call me."

"I promise," I said and watched her go.

I should have gone, too, but instead I stayed another hour at the bar. Finally, when the first wave of the office workers from the surrounding business washed in, I asked for the check, paid it and left.

□

I put the key into the lock, turned it, pushed the door and nothing happened. The dead-bolt was bolted. I fumbled on my key chain for the dead-bolt key and jammed it into the lock. I leaned my shoulder against the door and pushed. It opened. I stood for a moment staring at the door. I didn't remember bolting it. In fact, I never did.

Stepping into my apartment I suddenly stopped. There was something wrong. I looked around. Everything appeared as it had been when I set off for the university that morning, but was it? Had I closed the book lying on the coffee table? I walked around the room.

The dead-bolt. I knew I hadn't bolted the door. There was no point. There were so many other ways to break into my apartment that it never occurred to me that someone might try using the front door. But someone had, and he had very carefully turned both locks when he left.

Slowly, starting with my bedroom, I methodically went through every room of the apartment, taking inventory. It took more than an hour to make the search. In the bedroom, I lifted from the wall my framed law school diploma. I opened the wall safe beneath. There I found intact my grandfather's pocket watch, my birth certificate, my passport, my parents' wedding rings — optimistically bequeathed to me — and five thousand dollars cash, some of the bills twenty years old, the sum of my father's estate. Everything was accounted for.

It was the same in the bathroom and the kitchen and in the hall closet. I sat down at my desk and began going through the drawers. Then I discovered what was missing: Hugh's letters to his grandfather, which Aaron Gold had given me.

I closed the bottom drawer. Robert Paris was dead but someone had stolen the only evidence I had which linked him to the murder of his grandson. The apartment seemed suddenly very quiet. I felt as if I were in the presence of ghosts. As much to get out as to learn whether she'd seen or heard anything I went to my neighbor.

I pushed the doorbell beneath her name, Lisa Marsh. She came to the door in a bathrobe. This was not unusual, since she was a resident at the university medical school and worked odd hours. But her face was flushed, her hair disheveled and her eyes bright; it wasn't the appearance of sleep.

"Hi," I began, waiting for recognition to register with her.

She smiled.

"Sorry to get you out of bed but someone broke into my house this afternoon."

She stepped back. "Oh, no. When?"

"I left at ten this morning and got back an hour ago." I looked at my watch. It was about six. "I was wondering if you'd seen or heard anything."

"You better come in," she said. I did, closing the door behind me. All the curtains were drawn, but a lamp shone in a corner, revealing the remnants of a meal for two people laid out on a long coffee table. "Excuse me for a minute, Henry."

She went into her bedroom, and I heard her talking to someone. A few minutes later she returned with a man who was stuffing his shirttails into his jeans.

"I don't think you've met Mark," she said.

"Um, how do you do?" I said.

He smiled. "Fine."

"I am really sorry to disturb you," I said to both of them.

Lisa shrugged. "This is an emergency. Have you called the police?"

"No, not yet. I'm trying to figure out what happened first."

We went into the living room and sat down. I told them about the dead-bolt, the neatness of the search and the fact that only one thing had been taken. They did not ask, and I did not tell them, exactly what that thing was.

"What I was thinking," I concluded, "was that you may have heard something or seen someone."

They looked at each other and then back to me.

"We had lunch at around noon," Lisa said, "and were done by twelve-thirty. I'm afraid that after that we weren't paying much attention."

Mark frowned thoughtfully. "Wait. I heard a phone ringing next door. It woke me, and I looked over at the alarm clock thinking it might be the hospital — I work there, too. It was about three-thirty or a little before. Then I got up to use the bathroom and get a glass of water from the kitchen."

"Did you hear anything else?"

He shook his head.

The three of us looked at each other. Lisa touched her finger to her lip.

"But I did," she said. "The sound of silver rattling as somone opened a drawer. But I thought it was Mark."

"No, I got a glass from the counter. I didn't open any drawers."

"All this happened around three-thirty?"

"I'm sure of it," Mark said, "because I had to check in with the hospital at four."

I got up to leave. It was six-thirty. The burglar had been in my apartment only three hours earlier.

"What did he take?" Lisa asked.

"Some letters."

"Were they important?"

"The fact that they were stolen makes them important again," I said, then thanked them for their help.

Back in my apartment I headed for the phone. I hadn't noticed earlier that the answering machine had been shut off. I switched it back on. The recording dial was turned to erase. I moved the dial back to rewind, listening as the tape sped backwards. The message had not been rewound before my visitor attempted to erase it. Consequently, he had only succeeded in erasing blank tape. I turned the dial to play. There was the noise of someone trying to clear his throat and then the voice of a very drunk Aaron Gold.

"Henry . . . secretary said you called the other day . . . need to talk to you . . . s'important . . . s'about Hugh . . . Judge Paris . . . you got it wrong. Remember, no cops. I'm at home." The line went dead. I fast forwarded the tape to see if he'd called again. There were no other calls.

Mark said he heard the phone ringing at about three-thirty. A few minutes later, Lisa heard someone in my kitchen. Aaron's call must have come in while the burglar was in the apartment. If he was in the kitchen, which was just a few feet from the phone, the burglar heard the message. In fact, he not only tried to erase the message but turned the machine off so that the red light wouldn't immediately attract my attention. Shutting off the machine had also prevented any further messages from Aaron. Suddenly, I was very worried for him.

The phone rang at Aaron's house three times before his answering machine clicked on. I waited for the message to finish knowing that Aaron often screened his calls, and hoping that he was doing that now.

"Aaron, this is Henry," I said, practically shouting, "if you're at home, pick up the phone." The tape ran on. I tried calling his office but was told he hadn't been in that day. I put the phone down, got my car keys and hurried out of the apartment.

☐

Aaron lived in a small wooden house on Addison, set back from the road by a rather gloomy yard that was perpetually shaded by two massive oaks. There was a deep porch across the front of the house. The overhanging roof was supported by four squat and massive pillars completely out of proportion to the rest of the building. Gold and I referred to the place as Tara. The recollection of that mild joke dispelled some of my uneasiness as I opened the gate and stepped into the yard.

It was dusk and the shadows were at their deepest. Aaron's brown BMW was parked, a little crookedly, in the driveway. There were lights on behind the drawn curtains but the house was still. I heard a noise, a movement on the side of the house in the narrow strip of yard between the building and the fence that bounded the property.

Abruptly I stopped, turned and sped toward the side yard, moving as quietly as I could. When I reached the edge of the building I stopped and listened. Another noise, fainter. Breathing? I slowed my own breath. Someone had been coming up the side yard when he heard me open the gate. Now he was standing still, wondering, as I had wondered, at the source of the noise. I crouched, walked to the very edge of the building, and then sprang.

For an instant no longer than a heartbeat we saw each other through the evening shadows. He raised his arm to his chest, holding something in his hand. I balled my hand into a fist and brought it down on his wrist as hard as I could. Startled, he dropped what I now saw was a gun. He gasped, turned, and started running. I stooped down, retrieved the gun and ran after him. He was scrambling over the redwood fence when I got to the back yard.

"Stop," I shouted, training the gun at his back. I squeezed the trigger and then released it. It seemed suddenly darker as a burst of adrenilin rushed to my head. He was wearing — what? — dark pants, a dark shirt, taking the wall like an athlete. I knew that in another second it would be too late to stop him. I had to stop him. But shoot him? I was going to shoot a man? This wasn't even remotely a situation of self-defense. I held on to the gun and ran for the fence. He was nearly over the top. With my free hand, I reached up and grabbed his ankle. He kicked free. In another second I heard him drop to the ground on the other side. I clambered up the fence, trying to get footholds on the rough wood. Reaching the top, I looked down at the alley, which ran the length of the street. He was gone. He had run to the end of the block or else had gone into someone's back yard. I let myself drop back. Try to remember his face, I thought, as I made my way back to the house. The back door was ajar.

I entered the house through the kitchen.

"Aaron," I said in a whisper.

There was no answer. I groped for a light switch, found it and turned it on. The fluorescent light blinked on, filling the room with a white electric glare. From the doorway of the kitchen I could see into the dining room and to the arched entrance that led into the living room. There was a light on in there. I stepped into the dining room and repeated Aaron's name. There was no answer.

I crossed the room to the archway, holding the gun loosely at my side. Aaron Gold slumped forward in a brown leather arm-chair, his chest on his knees, his fingertips scraping the floor. Blood dripped steadily from his lap to a bright circle beneath him. On the table beside the chair was an empty bottle of Johnny Walker Red, a glass, and a small pitcher of water. The strongest smell in the room was of alcohol.

He'd probably been too drunk to know what was happening. I took no comfort from this.

I started toward him. There was a loud noise out on the porch, the sound of footsteps and voices. Someone was pounding on the door.

"This is the police. Mr. Gold. Open up. This is the police."

Numbly I went to the door and pulled it open. A young officer was flanked by three other cops. I opened my mouth to speak, but before I could utter a word, one of them said, "He's got a gun."

As soon as the sentence was out, there were four guns on me.

"Drop it," the first officer said. I let the gun slip from my hand to the floor. "Now step outside nice and easy."

"All right," I said, regaining my composure, "but my friend is hurt in there."

"We'll take care of him in a minute." One of the other officers directed me to turn, put my hands up against the wall and spread my legs. The felony position. I did as I was told. Another of the officers stepped into the house and I heard him mutter, "Jesus Christ." To the officers outside he said, "Get the para-medics."

I was searched, handcuffed and ordered to remain standing against the wall.

"This is a mistake," I said to the officer watching me.

"It sure is," he replied.

Now I heard the shriek of sirens as the paramedics' unit shat-tered the stillness of the night. I had often heard that noise and wondered to what tragedy they were being summoned. This time I knew.

The officer who had first come to the door approached me, pen and pad in hand.

"What's your name?"

"Henry Rios," I said.

He looked me over. Perhaps out of deference to the fact that I was still wearing most of my suit from the funeral, he called me mister.

"I'm going to read you your constitutional rights. Listen up." He began to read from the Miranda card in the dull drone that I had heard so many times before when I was a public defender. I had about fifteen seconds in which to make up my mind whether to talk to him or not.

"Do you understand these rights?" he was asking.

"Yes," I replied.

"Do you want a lawyer?"

"I am a lawyer," I said.

The answer startled him and then he searched my face carefully. "I've seen you before," he said.

"I was a public defender."

He whistled low beneath his breath. "Then you know the script," he said. "Do you want a lawyer?"

"Yes. Sonny Patterson at the D.A.'s office. I'll talk to him."

He nodded. "We're going to take you down to county," he said. "I'll radio ahead and have them rouse Patterson."

"Thank you."

He turned to one of his fellow-officers. "Take him."

"What charge?" the other asked.

"One eighty-seven," the first officer replied. Penal Code section 187 — murder.

Out in the street the paramedics had arrived.

— 9 —

It took Sonny Patterson two hours and seven phone calls to get me out of jail. Most of the time I sat on one of the three bunks in a holding cell watching soundless reruns of *Fantasy Island* while he wheedled on the phone in the booking office for my release.

The last time I'd been at county was as a public defender the morning I met Hugh Paris. Nothing at the jail had changed, including the inmate population. Several trusties who recognized me from back then drifted past the cell, not saying anything but just to stare. I smiled and said hello and they moved on.

The sheriffs let me keep my own clothes but they did not spare me any other part of the booking process. I was strip-searched, photographed, finger-printed and locked up, all the while thinking, this is unreal. The worst part was the strip-search. Until then it had never occurred to me to make the distinction between nudity and nakedness. Now I knew. Nudity was undressing to shower, or sleep, or make love. When you stripped in a hot closet-sized cell that smelled of the previous fifty men and under the indifferent stare of four cops, then you were naked. I still felt that nakedness. It was like a rash; I couldn't stop rubbing my body.

I made my mind into a blank screen across which flickered the images of the day from Robert Paris's casket to Aaron Gold's fingertips dipped in a dark pool of his own blood. These pictures passed through me like a shudder, but it was better than trying to suppress them.

This entire affair began with the murder of one man, Hugh Paris. Now it was assuming the dimensions of a massacre. No one connected with the Paris family seemed safe, including, perhaps, Robert Paris himself. Had the judge's death been purely coincidental to the fact that I'd begun to develop evidence that implicated him with three murders? Was there a gray eminence in the shadows directing events, or did the dead hand of Robert Paris still control the lethal machinery? Until that afternoon I had believed the investigation into Hugh's death was closed. The killing of Aaron Gold changed all that. I was back at the starting line, but with this difference: I was exhausted.

I lay back on the bunk and closed my eyes. Maybe it was the ever-present atmosphere of sexual tension in the jail or just my own loneliness, but I thought back to the last time Hugh and I had made love. Once again I saw the elegant torso stretched out beneath me as I lowered my body to his, and felt that body responding, resisting, yielding. The image of his face came to me with such clarity that I could see the fine blond hairs that grew, almost invisibly, between his eyebrows. And I could see his eyes and in those eyes I saw, with more regret than horror, the face of Aaron Gold bathed in blood.

I sat up. Sonny Patterson was watching me from just outside the cell.

"You all right?"

"Yeah, I must have fallen asleep."

"You look bad, pal."

"I've had better days." I rose from the bunk and walked to where he was standing. "Well?"

"It didn't look so good at first. Two shots fired from the gun, and your fingerprints all over the place. Fortunately for you, the same neighbor who called the cops also saw the guy going into the yard, and it wasn't you."

"Saw the guy?"

"Well, saw a guy. Blond, about your height. Good build. Good looking. Couldn't be you."

"I do what I can."

He lit a cigarette and offered me one. I hesitated and then accepted it. The last time I smoked I was eighteen.

"Incidentally, does that description sound like anyone you know?"

I shook my head.

"What about the guy you saw on the side of the house?"

I took a puff. It went down pretty smoothly. "It happened too fast. All I really saw was the gun."

"You're sounding like a witness for the prosecution. How come your defense witnesses always had such better memories?"

"Clean living, Sonny," I said, dropping the cigarette to the floor and crushing it with my heel. The second drag had made me want to vomit.

"Well, that's something I'll never be accused of." He smiled. "Hey, Wilson," he yelled to one of the jailers, "release the gentleman. He owes me a couple of drinks."

"I owe you a case."

"No," he said, suddenly serious. "You owe me an explanation."

"Did you call Terry Ormes?"

"Yeah, she's up in my office. That's where we're going."

□

It was only around ten but if felt like midnight. Sonny brewed a pot of coffee and brought out a fifth of Irish whiskey from the deep recesses of his desk. Terry yawned, accepted coffee but laid her hand across the cup when he started to pour the whiskey in. He shrugged and poured me a half-cup of coffee, a half-cup of whiskey. For himself, he dispensed with the coffee.

"Now that we're all comfortable," he began, settling into his armchair and his affected Southern drawl, "why don't you begin at the beginning?"

Between the two of us, Terry and I told Patterson the history of the Linden-Smith-Paris clan from the end of the nineteen twenties to the burial of Robert Paris that very afternoon. Patterson listened without comment, moving only to lower the level of fluid in the whiskey bottle now and then. There wasn't a lot left when we finished.

He looked back and forth between us and shrugged. "So," he said, "what crime has been committed that I can prove?"

Terry looked at him. "How about four murders, a burglary, and conspiracy to obstruct justice?"

"A crime that I can prove," he repeated. "In the murders of

Christina and Jeremy Paris, the eyewitness is dead, the coroner is dead, and the deaths have the appearance of being an accident. The remaining evidence — the will — is grist for speculation but not nearly enough to make out a murder. And the trail is twenty years old. The officers who wrote these reports might be dead themselves, and you know as well as I do that their reports are inadmissible hearsay. The death of Hugh Paris—" he glanced over at me. I'd told him that Hugh and I were lovers. "Put out of your head how much you liked the guy. Let me put it as crudely as I can — a hype O.D.'s and drowns. No one sees the death, no traces of murder survive except in Ormes's recollection. So maybe we can impute a motive to the judge, after a lot of circumstantial fandangoes, but so what? The judge is dead. Even assuming he arranged Hugh's murder, I doubt very seriously that he jotted it down in his appointment book." He looked at us.

"Aaron," I said.

"Yes, Aaron Gold. After I persuade the cops that you didn't do it — and you didn't, did you—?" I shook my head, "what do you think they're gonna conclude?"

"A break-in," Terry said wearily, "that got out of hand." Contemptuously, she added, "All the pieces fit."

"Detective," Patterson said, "cops are like prosecutors in this respect: we have to play the facts we're dealt. We can't engage in cosmic theories, because we're bound by the evidence we gather and the inferences we can draw from it. You can't expect me to put Robert Paris on trial for a murder that was committed four days after he died. All that the evidence will support in the case of Aaron Gold is a bungled burglary."

"The perfect crimes," Terry muttered.

"Exactly," Patterson said, shaking the last drops of liquor out of the bottle, "the perfect crimes. No witnesses, no evidence. Plenty of motive — if the murders could be connected, but nothing connects them except a few bits of circumstantial evidence and one hell of a lot of conjecture." He looked at us again and sighed. "Drink up."

"Drink up? Is that the D.A.'s position on these murders?"

"Jesus Christ, Henry, think of this case as a defense lawyer. Wouldn't you love to be defending Robert Paris? With the case I have against him?"

"Paris didn't physically kill Hugh, and he didn't pull the trigger on Aaron," I said. "The murderer is still alive."

"Then bring him to me," Patterson said, "and we'll talk."

I said, "This is a police matter."

Patterson shook his head. "You know as well as I do that the police don't have the time or interest to pursue this investigation. They've got their hands full. And as for you," he said, turning to Terry, "my advice is that if you place any value on your career on the force, you'll discontinue your interest in closed cases."

She lifted her eyebrows. "What do you mean?"

"I mean Hugh Paris," Patterson said. "I've been known to bend elbows with Sam Torres. He knows that you've been assisting Rios, and he doesn't like it. In fact, he considers it a personal affront that his subordinate would use police resources on a case that he closed and on behalf of a civilian."

"Christ," I muttered. Terry looked stricken and I knew why. A woman detective, even a good one — no, especially a good one — would always be walking the line. A misstep could have disastrous consequences on her career. I couldn't ask her to risk it for me.

"You're on your own, Henry," Patterson said. "Take my advice and forget it. Go away until things cool down. You're not safe."

"Then you believe the murders are all connected?"

"Of course I do. I believe every word of it. The rich are malignant." He held out his empty coffee cup to me. "Now what about those drinks?"

□

I woke late the next day, having closed a bar with Patterson the night before. Terry had begged off early. Sonny and I remained, getting drunk, swapping trial stories and he complaining about his marriage. Boys' night out, except that Aaron Gold was dead.

I went out for the papers. The San Francisco *Chronicle* made no mention of the murder, but the local daily put it on page one. I read it while the coffee brewed — burglary suspect, unidentified man detained and then released, no other suspects, would anyone having any information kindly notify the police.

As I drank my coffee, I wondered who there was to mourn Aaron. His law firm associates? A few ex-girlfriends? He had family in L.A. that he had spoken of maybe twenty times in all the years I'd known him. After all those years and all the people he'd known, I probably was still his closest friend. It disturbed me to think that he'd gone through life so alone. That image of opulent self-worth that he projected to the world was shadow play. My grief was real.

I needed to think, but the effort was painful; all the easy connections between Hugh's death and Aaron's led to a dead man, the judge. But there it was. Aaron had information he wanted to share with me about Hugh's death. The man who broke into my house was also interested in that information — not gaining access to it — but suppressing it. He also had taken the only proof I had linking Robert Paris to his grandson's death, so I'd assumed that Aaron's information further implicated the judge. But the judge was dead. What difference would it make to anyone whether his reputation was ruined?

And then it came to me. No one cared about the judge at this point. The break-in and Aaron's murder were the acts of someone with something left to lose should it become public knowledge that the judge had arranged his grandson's death. And who was that someone? Hugh's actual killer — the man or men hired by the judge to carry out the murder. Robert Paris's death hadn't really solved the crime. Hugh's murderer was still at large and I believed that that person was more than a goon employed for the occasion but someone upon whom the judge had relied pretty often. Who would know about the inner-workings of Paris' staff? Only a peer who had frequent dealings with that staff. John Smith.

And who was John Smith?

I had done a little research on Smith, gleaning the few facts I knew about him from the back issues of the *Chronicle* and my conversations with Grant. He was eighty-one years old, unmarried, a banker by profession, and something of a philanthropist. Four months out of the year he lived in Geneva where he was associated with various banks headquartered there. He was also chairman of the Linden Trust and, by virtue of his control of the disbursements of that fund, was more responsible for the development and course of nuclear research than any other private citizen. He gave money to Catholic charities, had had a rose named in his honor, had never graduated from college. In virtually every respect his life was opposite that of his brother-in-law, Robert Paris. Yet Smith, who lived in relative anonymity, was by birth something that Robert Paris never became, a member of the American aristocracy.

Nor, apparently, did the two men like each other. There was never anything as obvious as a public falling out. As stewards of the Linden fortune, their economic interests frequently converged and were too important to allow personal feelings to stand in the way of greater enrichment. Nonetheless, Grant had spoken as if the enmity between the two ancient tycoons was public knowledge.

All this made Smith a potential ally. Someone in Robert Paris's retinue had killed Hugh and Aaron. I could not interest the police in pursuing the investigation but Smith, with his money and influence, could. What remained was to make an appeal to him. I needed entree into his world. Once again I would have to rely on Grant Hancock whose family, though perhaps poorer, was as distinguished as Smith's.

I picked up the phone and dialed Grant's number.

Grant was at work. I reached his secretary who made it clear to me that unless I was a paying client I could leave a message. Finally, after lengthy negotiation, she agreed to give Mr. Hancock my name. He was on the phone a moment later.

"Henry, I was going to call you. I just heard a very disturbing rumor about Aaron from one of our classmates who was working on a case with him."

"It's true, Grant. Aaron's been murdered."

"Jesus."

"And I was arrested for his murder and spent half the night in jail."

"What?"

"And the same day he was murdered, someone broke into my apartment and stole the letters that Hugh had written to his grandfather. Aaron called my apartment while the break-in was in progress. He said he had information about Hugh's death. Whoever was in my apartment — and I think it was Hugh's killer — heard the phone message and tried to erase it. Then the killer went to Aaron's. When I got to Aaron's house, he was dead."

"Wait — Hugh's killer killed Aaron? The judge killed Hugh."

"No, the judge had Hugh killed. An important distinction, Grant. The man who did the actual killing is still at large and probably in a panic since the death of his employer."

"Didn't you also just say you'd been arrested for Aaron's murder?"

"Yes."

"How did that happen?"

"I was holding the gun." I heard Grant make a noise, and I explained how it was I came to be at Aaron's house when the police arrived. I also told him that the police were treating the case as a burglary and that the district attorney considered any other interpretation of the events leading to Aaron's death unprovable.

"But you think differently."

"Yes."

"I was afraid of that. I take it, then, this is not a social call."

"Grant, I've respected your wish to be left out of this, until now."

"Is that the sound of chips being cashed I hear?" he said.

"The police are prepared to write off Aaron's death the same way they wrote off Hugh," I continued, ignoring his joke. "I want to make contact with John Smith."

"You're obsessed with Smith," Grant said. "He's just a private citizen — albeit a rich one."

"Money makes things happen," I replied, "and if even you feel intimidated by John Smith, imagine his effect on a chief-of-police. Or the mayor."

There was a thoughtful silence on the line.

"First," Grant said, "you'll have to engage his attention."

"All I want is my foot in the door."

"I'm going to put you on hold," Grant said, and the line went blank. Five minutes later he came back on. "Sorry," he said, "I had to make a call. I want you to call this number and ask for Peter Barron. He's one of Smith's aides at Pegasus."

"At what?"

"Pegasus. Smith's corporate flagship. A holding company."

He gave me the number. I thanked him. We hung up.

A company that owns companies. That's how Terry Ormes had described the corporation that held title to the house in San Francisco that Hugh had leased and was living in at the time of his death. Pegasus Corporation.

I dialed the number Grant had given me.

"Good morning. Mr. Barron's office," a woman said.

"Is Mr. Barron in?"

"Yes. Who may I say is calling?"

"Henry Rios."

"May I tell Mr. Barron what this call is in reference to?"

"Hugh Paris," I replied.

"One moment." I was back on hold.

"Good morning, Mr. Rios," a male voice said. For the briefest moment I thought I recognized the voice.

"Mr. Barron? I'm a friend of Grant Hancock. He gave me your number—"

"How is Grant?"

"He's fine. Look, I have some information about Hugh Paris's death that I think might interest your employer, Mr. Smith."

"Such as?"

"Hugh was murdered at the direction of his grandfather, Robert Paris, and whoever performed the killing is still at large."

There was a long skeptical pause. "I see," he said finally. "Have you shared this information with the police?"

"The police take the position that Hugh's death was accidental."

"Oh, is that the position the police take?" His tone was mocking. Once again, his voice sounded familiar. "Well, Mr. Rios, I doubt that Mr. Smith is in any position to do what the police can't or won't do. He was deeply affected by Hugh's death, and I think, at his age, he should be spared these speculations which would only make Hugh's loss harder to accept."

"It's not speculation. I have proof."

"Mr. Rios, give the old man a break. He doesn't need to hear that members of his family killed each other off. Take your story back to the police or, better yet, keep it to yourself."

Switching to a different tack I asked, "Who arranged for the lease of Hugh's house from Pegasus?"

"What are you talking about?"

"Hugh leased his house from Pegasus. Who was his contact there?"

"Pegasus isn't in the real estate business."

"I saw the lease."

There was silence on the other end. At last he said, "Can't be. Look, Henry, I really must go."

"Have we ever met?"

"I don't think so," he replied, sounding, I thought, nervous.

"I know your voice."

"Well, maybe we've met through Grant. Goodbye, Henry."

The line went dead.

A moment later I was back on the phone to Grant asking him what Peter Barron looked like.

"I've only seen him a few times. He's about our age. Blond. Handsome. Gay."

Blond, good-looking — that's how Aaron's neighbor described the man he saw in Aaron's yard the night of the murder. Was that also the man I saw? I closed my eyes, but I was unable to picture the face. Still, his hair — it was blond, wasn't it? And I knew I had seen him somewhere before.

"Gay?" I asked Grant. This, too, seemed significant.

"I've run into him at Sutter's Mill," he said, naming a bar popular with professionals. "Did he say something to you?"

"No, nothing like that. Is there any chance I might've met him through you?"

"I hadn't seen you in four years until two weeks ago," Grant said. "Hardly enough time to introduce you to my friends, much less a cocktail party acquaintance. Do you know Peter Barron?"

"I'm sure of it, but I can't figure out where. He knows we've met, too. He lied to me about that and about Hugh's relation to Pegasus. I think I'd better drive up to the city. Where is Pegasus?"

Grant gave me an address on Montgomery Street.

"I'll call you," I said and hung up.

□

Pegasus Corporation was housed on floors thirty-eight, thirty-nine and forty of a Japanese bank building near the Embarcadero freeway. I called up to Barron's office from the street to make sure he was in, then I entered the building. It was close to noon and I explained to the security guard that I was meeting someone for a lunchtime conference but had misplaced his office number. I gave the guard Peter Barron's name and he made a call.

"He's on thirty-nine, sir," the guard said. "Take one of the elevators to your right."

On the thirty-ninth floor I played a variation of the same trick with the receptionist, a stern-looking young Chinese woman who sat at a desk beneath a large brass engraving of Pegasus in flight.

"Hello. Do you know if Mr. Barron's gone out to lunch yet?"

She glanced at a sheet of paper. "No," she said, reaching for the phone. "You have an appointment?"

"Wait," I said, briefly laying my hand over hers as she touched the phone. "Peter and I roomed together in college ten years ago and I haven't seen him since. I'm in town for the week and wanted to surprise him. Understand?"

She nodded.

"Do you know when he goes out to lunch?"

"Any minute now. You can wait here."

"Okay, but — well, when I saw Peter he still had hair to his shoulders and was as skinny as a pole. I'm not sure I'd recognize him."

She nodded again as gravely as if I were administering a quiz. Or maybe it was my antiquity that intimidated her. Her own college years could hardly be more than a few months behind her.

"Can you describe him to me?" I asked.

She looked at the wall behind me, thinking. "He's about six

feet," she began hesitantly, "blond hair and blue eyes. Nice build." She giggled. "Very handsome."

Her description added nothing to what Grant had already told me and it fit about ten thousand men in the financial district alone.

"Thank you," I said. "I'll sit here with a magazine pulled up over my face and wait for Peter. You just carry on with your job. All right?"

"All right," she said and answered a call.

I looked at my watch. It was twelve-five. Six minutes later, behind a flock of secretaries, a blond man stepped into the room from a door beside the receptionist's desk. I recognized him at once. He informed the receptionist that he would be out for the rest of the day.

She replied loudly, "Thank you, Mr. Barron."

He started walking out into the corridor. I put my magazine down and fell into step beside him.

"Hello, Peter."

He glanced at me and stopped. "Henry. I was just going to pay you a visit."

He spoke in the same soft reasonable tone of voice with which he had addressed me only three weeks earlier, the night he and his three friends abducted me as I was leaving Grant Hancock's apartment and shot me up with sodium pentothal. Peter was the one who wielded the needle and told me he wanted information for his employer, who I had then thought was Robert Paris.

"You work for Smith," I said.

"You're surprised?"

"It doesn't make sense to me, especially if you also killed Aaron Gold."

"Killed who?"

"You killed Hugh Paris and you killed Aaron Gold."

"Henry," he said with a small, hurt smile. "I have never killed anyone and as for our last meeting, you might at least give me a chance to explain."

"One doesn't explain away two murders."

He sighed impatiently, "Damn it, Henry, I don't know what you're talking about. All right, Hugh was murdered, but not by me. This other guy I've never even heard of."

My curiosity overcame me. "Then who killed Hugh?"

He shook his head. "We — Mr. Smith and I — have been try-ing to find out. I don't know. That's why I — what did you call it — abducted you — that night."

I looked at him. We were standing in the corridor while people rushed around us. He seemed calm and rational for someone just accused of two murders. I, by contrast, was beginning to sound hysterical even to myself. And he worked for Smith. Smith, in my scheme of things, was a good guy.

Perhaps sensing my uncertainty he said, "There's a lot I have to tell you about Hugh's death, Henry, and you have the most urgent right to know. You were his lover."

"How did you know that?" I demanded.

"We've been working the same field. You know about me. I know about you." He reached out and laid a hand on my shoulder. "I'm gay, too, Henry. I understand."

I didn't want to believe him but no one, not even Grant, had acknowledged my right to grieve. The weight of Hugh's death and the frustration I felt at not knowing who killed him all closed in on me. I brushed aside a tear. Barron tactfully looked away.

"All right," I said. "Let's go somewhere and talk."

We walked to an elevator and stepped inside.

"What exactly do you do for Smith?" I asked.

He reached his hand into his jacket, pulling out a gun.

"Special assignments," he replied. "Now, we're going down to the garage, and then we'll get off, you first with me following. You behave yourself, Henry, and maybe I'll let you live."

I looked into his eyes, felt his breath on my face. He smiled and then stepped behind me, against the wall of the elevator.

"You're crazy," I said. "You killed Hugh and Aaron Gold."

"An interesting thought," he said. "But why would I've done that? Who was I working for?"

"Maybe no one," I replied. "You might just be a freelance psychopath."

"Let's not call names," he said nudging the nozzle of the gun into the small of my back.

At that moment the elevator stopped. A dozen people crowded on. The gun pressed harder against my back.

I clenched my hands into fists. "This man's got a gun," I shouted and jerked away from Barron.

A woman screamed.

"Get him," someone shouted.

The elevator stopped again. The doors flew open. Barron pushed his way to the front as hands reached out trying to stop him. He broke clean and ran down the corridor. Perhaps aware that he was still armed, no one followed. The elevator door closed.

"Who was he?" a man asked me.

"A nut with a gun," I replied.

Three hours later I was sitting on the floor in Grant Hancock's apartment drinking a glass of wine while he went to the door to pay for a delivery of Chinese food. He took the small white cartons from a brown bag and set them on a tea tray between us. We opened them up and ate from them with wooden chopsticks.

I had just told him that after getting the names of the other people on the elevator I'd gone to the police.

"What did they do?"

"What cops always do, they took a report and promised to look into it. By the time that report reaches the appropriate desk, Peter Barron could be in Tierra del Fuego."

Grant chewed a bit of shrimp.

"I don't understand why Barron pulled a gun on you. He works for Smith. Smith is supposed to be on our side."

"Does he work for Smith? I mean, he does, ostensibly, but in actuality I think he was working for Robert Paris."

"That sounds complicated."

"But it fits the evidence. What I think happened is that Hugh contacted Smith to let Smith know he was back in town. Maybe he even enlisted Smith's help in exposing Robert Paris as the murderer of Christina and Nicholas. Smith leased the house for him, probably gave him money. Peter Barron works for the security section of Pegasus — I think Smith might have entrusted him to keep an eye on Hugh and make sure he stayed out of trouble. In fact, I remember that it was Smith who bailed Hugh out of jail when he was arrested in July."

"Are you positive?"

"Yes, I called the jail and had them check." I finished my wine and poured another glass. "At the time I thought John Smith was an alias used to avoid notoriety by whoever bailed Hugh out."

"Well, it is hard to believe there are men in the world actually named John Smith."

I poked at the carton of rice.

"Anyway," I continued, "Barron was supposed to protect Hugh but instead he betrayed him to Robert Paris."

"How would Barron have known about the bad blood between Hugh and Robert Paris?"

"I'm sure Hugh told him," I said. "It was a subject to which he often returned."

Grant nodded.

"So Barron went to Robert Paris with the information that Hugh was in the city and that he, Barron, knew where Hugh was. Paris then paid Barron to murder Hugh. And that's how it was done."

"And Smith? Don't you think he was a little suspicious about the circumstances of Hugh's death?"

"I'm sure he was. He probably had Barron conduct an investigation. You can imagine Barron's conclusion."

Grant put down the carton from which he'd been eating. "And Aaron? Why kill Aaron?"

"Aaron worked for the firm that handled Paris's legal work. He must've learned something very damaging that implicated Barron with Hugh's murder."

"Such as?"

"Pay-offs, maybe. Reports. I don't know. Aaron never had a chance to tell me."

"How much of this do you think Smith knows?" Grant asked, pouring me the last of the wine.

"My impression of Smith from reading the newspapers," I said, "is that information reaches him through about three dozen intermediaries. Everything is sanitized by the time it touches his desk. He probably knows next to nothing about what really went on."

"And you're going to tell him."

"Yes." I picked up a bit of chicken with my chopsticks. "It's strange that Hugh never talked to me about Smith."

"From everything you've said, it doesn't sound like Hugh told you much about his family."

"That's true."

"He wanted to protect you. Knowing how potentially dangerous the situation was, he wanted to keep you out of it." After a pause he added, "He loved you."

"Instead of protecting me, Hugh left me ignorant — and vulnerable."

Grant sighed. "When do we ever do the right thing by the people we love?"

When, indeed, I wondered, looking at him from across the room.

□

The next day I went back to Pegasus, this time to see Smith but I got no closer than his secretary. She, unlike the gullible receptionist, was not inclined to let strange men without appointments loiter in her office. She threatened to have me ejected. Taking the hint, I went out into the corridor to ponder my next move. There didn't seem to be any. Two middle-aged men in dark suits came out of Smith's office and passed. Their jowls quivered with self-importance. I watched them walk to a door at the end of the corridor — what I'd assumed was a freight elevator.

One of the two withdrew a key from his pocket and fit it into a lock on the wall. The door slid open, revealing a small plushly appointed elevator.

The executive elevator. Of course.

It would hardly do for Smith and his retinue to waste expensive time waiting for the public elevator or to endure the indignities of making small talk with file clerks. Smith would have to leave at some point, and, if I couldn't wait for him in his office, I'd wait here.

So I waited. I waited from ten in the morning to nearly six at night, fending off the occasional security guard with my business card and an explanation that I was meeting a friend from

Pegasus's legal staff. I thought that Smith might emerge for lunch until I saw a food-laden trolley wheeled off the executive elevator by a red jacketed waiter. About an hour later the waiter reappeared with the now empty trolley and boarded the elevator. Just as the doors closed I saw him finish off the contents of a wine glass.

At about four a few lucky employees began to leave, singly, or in groups of two or three. By five, the corridor was packed. By five-forty-five when it seemed that everyone who could possibly work at Pegasus had left for the day, the doors were pushed open and two beefy bodyguard-types strode out flanking a third man. The third man was tall, thin and old. The blue pinstriped suit he wore fell loosely on his frame and was shabby with many wearings, but he wore it as if it were a prince's ermine. They walked rapidly past me to the executive elevator. The key went into the lock. I rushed over to where they were standing.

"Mr. Smith."

The tall old gentleman turned toward me slowly, examining me without particular interest.

"My name is Henry Rios. I have to talk to you about Hugh Paris."

At the mention of my name, the old man raised his eyebrows a fraction of an inch, indicating, I thought, either recognition or surprise. However, he said nothing. The two men closed ranks in front of him.

"Don't come any closer," one of them said, allowing his jacket to fall open, revealing a shoulder holster.

John Smith's employees, it seemed, were issued sidearms along with their Brooks Brothers charge plates. I stepped back.

"All I want is ten minutes of your time," I said to Smith.

The elevator door opened and he stepped into it. The bodyguards followed him in. I lunged forward trying to keep the doors open. "Ten minutes," I shouted.

The same man who'd just spoken to me now lifted a heavy leg and booted me in the chest, throwing me backwards to the floor.

I lifted myself up.

John Smith was staring at me. He opened his mouth to speak just as the doors shut.

— 10 —

The wine was cold and bitter. A white-jacketed busboy moved through the darkness of the restaurant like a ghost. Outside, a freakish spell of blisteringly hot weather had emptied the streets but here it was cool and dark and the only noise was the murmur of conversation and the silvery clink of flatware against china, ice against glass. It was two o'clock in the afternoon. Aaron Gold had been buried that morning in Los Angeles.

Grant asked, "Should we have sent flowers?"

"I've never understood that custom," I replied. "Are the flowers intended as a symbol of resurrection or are they just there to divert attention from the corpse?"

But Grant wasn't listening. His glance had fallen to the front page of the *Chronicle* laid out on the table between us. The contents of Robert Paris's will had been made public. His entire estate, five hundred million dollars, was bequeathed to the Linden Trust of which John Smith was chairman. Would it matter to Smith now that Robert Paris was a murderer or was half a billion dollars sufficient reparation?

As if he read my thoughts, Grant looked up at me unhappily and said, "There's no justice in this. You must do something."

"I've tried everything," I said to Grant, "everything I could think of doing."

A waiter set down shallow bowls of steaming pasta before us. The fragrance of basil rose from the dish reminding me of summer. I picked up my fork.

"You haven't tried what you're trained to do," Grant said.

I lifted an interrogatory eyebrow.

"I've been thinking about this," Grant said. "The first thing you have to do is ask yourself what it is you want. You don't want the identity of the killer, you already know who that is, but what you do want is to bring the killer to justice. And I'm not talking about Barron — he was just the instrument — I'm talking about Robert Paris. You want there to be a public record of his guilt."

I nodded.

"Who is better able to make that record than a lawyer in a court of law?"

"Unfortunately," I said, "Judge Paris is no longer within any court's jurisdiction."

"Wrong," Grant said. "You're thinking of the criminal side."

I put my fork down. "What are you thinking of?"

"Well, I'm not a litigator, of course, but it occurred to me that you should sue him."

Grant picked up his fork and speared a clam. I watched him chew and swallow. My brain was buzzing. Why hadn't I thought of this before?

"Of course," I said. "Wrongful death. I'll sue Robert Paris's estate for the wrongful death of Hugh Paris."

"And Aaron too."

I shook my head. "The judge was already dead when that happened. We'd never be able to prove it."

Grant buttered a bit of bread. "You think we could prove it as to Hugh's death?"

"I don't know but we'll do a hell of a lot of damage to Robert Paris's reputation in the attempt."

I thought some more.

"In fact," I continued, "we can do some damage to John Smith while we're at it, or at least get his attention."

"How?"

"Well, if a suit is pending against Paris's estate which involves money damages, there should be enough money set aside from the estate to cover those damages in the event the suit succeeds."

Grant dabbed his mouth with a napkin and smiled.

"You mean we can obtain some kind of injunction to prevent the judge's executors from disbursing the estate."

"Exactly. The Linden Trust won't get a penny until the suit's resolved. And as for the executor," I continued, "which happens to be Aaron's law firm, we'll plaster them with discovery motions and compel them to produce every scrap of paper they have that involves Hugh or Peter Barron or Robert Paris. We'll depose everyone from the senior partner to the receptionist."

"Those depositions will make the front page of the *Chronicle*," he said.

"For months," I replied, "if not years." Smiling, I reached across the table and patted his head. "Good thinking for someone who's not a litigator. It's perfect, Grant."

Grant looked at me and smiled nervously. "Well, not quite perfect," he said. "As I understand it, the only people entitled to bring the suit would be Hugh's executors or his heirs."

It took a moment before I understood. "Katherine Paris."

"I'm afraid so," he said.

□

Katherine Paris lit a cigarette and eyed me suspiciously from across my desk. We were in my office. This was the first time I'd used it for business since I'd leased it three months earlier. There was a film of dust on the bookshelves and the file cabinets. Both were empty. The only objects of my desk were three newly purchased volumes of the code of civil procedure, the probate code and the evidence code, a yellow legal tablet, my pen and the plastic cup into which Mrs. Paris tapped her cigarette ash.

"Tell me again how this works," she said, "preferably in English. I cannot follow you when you start quoting the law at me."

I smiled as charmingly as I knew how. Her hard, intelligent face showed no sign of being charmed. I had virtually pulled her off a plane to Boston to get her to talk to me. Her baggage had gone on without her. Now she planned to leave that night on another flight. The clock was ticking away.

"It's called a wrongful death action," I said, "and it's a law suit brought by the heirs or estate of someone who died through the negligence or wrongful act of another. The most common instance is a suit brought by the family of someone killed in a car accident or on the job."

"I would hardly classify homicide as an instance of neglect," she remarked impatiently.

"But it is a wrongful act."

"Oh, at the very least," she snickered.

"Mrs. Paris, please — I know it sounds like hair-splitting, but there are precedents in the case law that permit the heirs of a murder victim to bring an action against his murderer."

"So you want my consent to bring this wrongful death action against Robert's estate."

"Exactly."

"And you intend to ask for two hundred and fifty million dollars in damages?"

"Yes."

She stubbed out her cigarette. "What you want is permission to conduct a circus."

I began to respond but she cut me off.

"Mr. Rios, you are a very clever man and I have no doubt that you were devoted to Hugh but this idea of yours is absurd."

"It's not absurd," I said, "It's entirely plausible." She remained unimpressed. "Mrs. Paris, you stand to gain by this suit whether we get to trial or not."

"What are you talking about?"

"I know that you were left nothing in Robert Paris's will. There's enough truth to this suit that even if we can't prove the allegation that the judge had Hugh murdered, the suit has considerable harassment value."

"I beg your pardon?"

"It takes five years to get a relatively simple civil lawsuit to trial. A case of this magnitude could drag on for a decade, easily. At some point the judge's executors will simply decide to pay you off and settle the suit."

"But what would you get out of that, Mr. Rios? Surely you have other motives for wanting to sue Robert's estate than my further enrichment."

"I intend to pursue this case through the pages of the *Chroni-*

cle so that even the fact of a settlement will be an admission of Robert Paris's guilt. That will satisfy me, Mrs. Paris," I said with rising emotion, "even if it takes the next ten years of my life to accomplish it."

Visibly startled by my vehemence, she sat back in her chair.

"It won't bring Hugh back to life," she said softly.

"Mrs. Paris, do you have any doubt that Hugh was murdered?"

"No," she said, without hesitation.

"And do you have any doubt that Robert Paris was his murderer?"

In a softer voice she said, "No."

"But the police say Hugh killed himself, shot himself full of heroin and drowned in three feet of water. You saw the body."

Her face went white. Her cigarette burned unheeded. She nodded.

"How can you allow your son to be slandered with this ridiculous explanation of his death? It's as if you left his body to the vultures. Doesn't he deserve a decent burial, a peaceful rest?"

"Spare me," she whispered.

"I can't," I said. "I loved him."

She lit another cigarette and proceeded to smoke it, all the while looking out the window as dusk gathered in the sky. Once she lifted a long finger to the ivory cameo at the neck of her blouse. Perhaps her husband had given it to her, perhaps, even, it had been given to her by Hugh. At length she turned her face back to me and studied me for a long time. I did not avoid her eyes but looked back into them.

"You loved him," she said, at last, echoing me. "I told you once I didn't understand that kind of love."

"That love differs only in expression but not quality from the love you felt for him."

"No," she said. "The quality is different. Yours — it's much finer."

"May I proceed with the suit?"

She said, "All right."

The words fell like two smooth pebbles and clattered on the desk between us.

"Thank you, Mrs. Paris."

"But I intend to catch that flight for Boston tonight. You'll be on your own."

"I understand that."

"Yes, I imagine you do," she said. "You strike me as someone who was born to be on his own. I know I was." These last words were spoken with sadness, resignation. Recovering herself, she said, "I suppose you want me to sign something."

"No," I said. "You'll either be good at your word or you won't. If not, a piece of paper won't compel you."

"You needn't worry about my word. I never give it unless I intend to honor it."

I nodded, slightly, in acknowledgment.

"However," she continued, "I wish to add one condition of your employment by me. You may take your thirty percent if and when we win. In the meantime—" she dug into her bag and withdrew a leather checkbook, "you'll need money to proceed."

I watched her write out a check for ten thousand dollars and lay it on the desk between us.

"I'll expect an accounting, of course," she said. "If you need more money notify me at the address on the check. But do remember, Mr. Rios, while I may be well-off I'm counting on you to make me truly rich, so spend wisely."

"I will."

She rose and gathered up her things. "Now tell me, Mr. Rios, truthfully, if we do get to trial what are our chances of winning?"

"Let me give you a legal answer," I said. "I would say we have two chances, fat and slim."

She let out a low, throaty laugh that echoed in the room even after she'd left.

□

The next morning I stepped up to the counter of the clerk of the superior court, wrote out a check, handed it over with a stack of papers to a young black woman, and with those actions commenced the suit of *Paris versus Paris*. Along with the complaint and summons, I filed a request for discovery and a restraining order against the disbursement of Robert Paris's estate pending the outcome of this action. Simultaneously, a courier service I'd hired with some of Mrs. Paris's money served copies of the documents upon Grayson, Graves and Miller as executors of the judge's estate. The clerk stamped my copies of the papers and handed them back to me, wishing me a good day as she did. I thanked her and stepped out into the hall and into the glare of television cameras.

"Sir, look this way, please," a voice called to me. I turned to the camera. A blond man in a gray suit spoke into a microphone, explaining that I had just filed a two hundred and fifty million dollar lawsuit against the estate of Robert Paris claiming that Paris had murdered his grandson. He spoke with no particular urgency and in a normal tone of voice, but to me it was as if he was shouting his words to the world through an amplifier on the tip of the Transamerica pyramid.

At length the blond, introducing himself as Greg Miller, turned to me and said, "Mr. Rios, why have you filed this lawsuit rather than going to the police?"

I cleared my throat and told my story.

□

When I woke the next morning the phone was already ringing. I let my answering machine take the message as I got out of bed and wandered into the kitchen to start the coffee. I caught the tail end of the message — a reporter from the L.A. *Times* requesting an interview.

I'd gotten to bed at three that morning, having spent the previous twelve hours talking to reporters from newspapers and television stations from Sacramento to Bakersfield. I put on a bathrobe and stepped outside to pick up the *Chronicle* and the local. I'd made the front page of both. I glanced at the stories — they were the usual jumble of fact and fantasy but the slant was decidedly in my favor.

I skimmed the rest of the *Chronicle*. On the next-to-the-last-page, in the society section, I saw a picture of John Smith. He'd attended a charitable function the night before and was shown arriving at the Fairmont. By his expression I saw that he was used to having his picture taken but not particularly tolerant of the practice. He looked away from the camera, both his eyes and his mind visibly occupied on another matter. I had a good idea of what it was.

I folded the paper across Smith's face and went to the window. Outside the sky was clouded over. Knots of red and yellow leaves waved back and forth in the trees like pennants. There was a lot to be done that day. Grant was expecting me for lunch where we would map out our litigation strategy. The phone messages would have to be responded to. I needed to hire a secretary and have a phone installed in my office. Abruptly, I had become a practicing lawyer. It felt good.

I rinsed out my coffee cup and went to the bedroom where I changed into my sweats and running shoes. I stretched in the living room for a couple of minutes and then went out. It was about seven and there weren't many other people on the road. A Chinese boy came flying by, long, skinny legs pounding the sidewalk, black hair flapping like silk at the back of his head. We nodded acknowledgment as we passed each other.

It had been some time since I'd last run and it took longer than usual to catch my stride. I swiveled my head back and forth, trying to relax my neck. It was then that I noticed the silver Rolls.

It was gliding a few feet behind me, too slowly and with too little sense of direction. I increased my speed and turned a corner. I looked over my shoulder, and it was still following. Suddenly, the car sped up, turned the corner ahead of me and stopped in my path. I slowed to a trot. The front passenger window was soundlessly lowered. I felt a surge of prickly heat across my chest as my blood rushed not from exertion but from fear. I stopped. The only person in the car was the driver. He was a middle-aged man with silver hair, wearing a black suit, white shirt, black tie and a visored black cap. He turned his face to me and smiled.

"Mr. Rios?" he called out. "I'm sorry if I startled you."

Cautiously, I approached the car close enough to talk without shouting.

"How do you know who I am?"

"Your picture's in the papers," he said. "Mr. Smith wonders if he could see you."

"John Smith?"

The driver nodded.

"Now?"

"Yes, sir."

I looked at him. He seemed harmless but then I couldn't see his lower body from where I was standing.

"And where does Mr. Smith propose we have this meeting?"

"He's waiting for you at the Linden Museum on the university campus."

"Step out of the car, please, and come around to my side."

"Sir?"

"Please."

I heard him sigh as he opened the door and got out. When he came around I told him to turn his back to me, put his hands on the top of the car, and spread his legs.

"Is this really necessary?" he asked as I patted him down for weapons.

"Don't take it personally," I replied, "but the last time I got into a small enclosed space with one of Mr. Smith's employees he pulled a gun on me."

"I'm not armed," the driver replied.

"So I see," I said, turning him around by the shoulders. "On the other hand you've got twenty pounds over me and it feels like muscle. Do you know where you are now in relation to the museum?"

"Yes."

I looked into the car and saw the key was in the ignition. "Then you won't mind walking there."

"Come now, Mr. Rios—" he began.

"Look," I said. "I'll drive myself to the museum alone, or I won't go at all. Understood?"

After a moment's pause, he said, "Understood. But be careful with the car."

"I hear they drive themselves," I said, getting into the driver's seat.

I calculated that it would take the driver at least a half hour to walk back to campus. Smith, or whoever had dispatched him, was probably not even certain I could be lured to the museum, much less at a fixed time, but he would begin to get nervous if too much time passed without word from the driver. I could cover the distance to the campus in about ten minutes. This gave me, I decided, about fifteen minutes of dead time before anyone got jittery. Fifteen minutes was more than enough time for the plan that now suggested itself to me.

I made a stop. When I started up again, ten minutes later, I noticed the white van a car-length behind me. I began to whistle. The van's lights flickered on and off. I relaxed.

I drove beneath the stone arch and onto Palm Drive. Just before I reached the oval lawn that fronted the Old Quad I turned off a rickety little side street called Museum Way. When I looked in my mirror, the van was gone. I followed the road for a few hundred yards until it ended, abruptly, at the voluminous steps of a sandstone building, the Grover Linden Museum of Fine Art. I parked the car and got out.

The edifice, reputedly inspired by St. Peter's, consisted of a domed central building and two wings jutting off on each side at a slight angle. As a law student, I had sometimes come here to study since it was as deserted a spot on campus as existed. It was deserted now as I made my way up the steps to where a uniformed university security guard stood. Behind him, the museum's hours were posted on the door and indicated, quite clearly, that the museum was closed on Tuesdays. Today was Tuesday.

"Mr. Rios?"

"That's right."

"Go right in, sir. Mr. Smith is up on the second floor in the family gallery. Do you know where that is?"

"Yes."

The monster was surprisingly graceful inside. Sunlight poured into the massive foyer from a glass dome in the ceiling. A beautiful staircase led up from the center of the foyer to the second floor. Walkways on that floor connected the right and left wings of the museum. The staircase and interior walls were white marble, the banisters of the staircase were polished oak and the railings were bronze. All that glare of white and polished surfaces made me feel that I was inside a wedding cake.

I started up the stairs to the second floor, got to the top and turned right. Above the entrance to the gallery at my right were chiseled the words "the Linden Family Collection." On each side of that entrance stood an armed security guard. They weren't wearing the university's uniforms. I stepped past them into the room.

The family gallery was a long and narrow rectangular room. Along one of the long walls were six tall windows looking out over a garden. Along the other were paintings of the various buildings of the university as they existed on the day the university opened its doors for business. There were also a dozen standing glass cases that displayed such memorabilia as Grover Linden's eyeglasses, Mrs. Linden's rosary and a collection of dolls belonging to the Linden's only daughter.

I strolled past these treasures toward the end of the room. There, alone on the wall, hung the only well-known work in the room, a six foot portrait of Grover Linden himself painted by John Singer Sargent. Beneath it, on a wooden bench, sat an old man, John Smith.

There was no one else in the room and the only noise was the soft squish of my running shoes as I walked across the marble floor. Smith rose as he saw me approach. At six foot four he had five inches over me but was thin and frail-looking. The tremulous light that fell across his face washed it of all color. Even his eyes were faded and strangely lifeless as if they'd already closed on the world. He extended his hand to me. His grip was loose and perfunctory and the hand itself skeletal and cold. And yet, even that touch conveyed authority. He sat down again and motioned me to sit beside him. I did. The two guards at the other end of the room moved to just inside the gallery. I felt their eyes on us.

"Thank you for coming," Smith said in a surprisingly firm voice. He elongated his vowels in the manner of Franklin Roosevelt, I noticed; the accent of wealth from an earlier time.

"You're welcome. Though I must say this is an odd meeting place."

"My lawyers," he said, "advised me not to speak to you at all, since it's likely that I'll become involved in this lawsuit of yours, but I had to talk to you."

"So we're hiding from your lawyers?"

"Exactly," he replied. We watched dust motes fall through the air. "You know I haven't been to this museum since it was dedicated sixty years ago. Of course I was just a boy then. But for years I dreamed about this portrait of my grandfather."

"Is it a fair likeness?"

"It errs on the side of tact," he said, smiling a little. He cleared his throat with a murmur. "Now, Mr. Rios, perhaps we can discuss our business."

"Which is?"

"This — lawsuit." He looked at me and said, "What will it cost me to persuade you to drop it?"

"Well, to begin with, an explanation of why you would make such a request."

"My family's good name," he said.

"Robert Paris was a member of your family by marriage only," I said, "and, from what I understand, no friend of yours. Additionally, my information is that he was responsible not only for the murder of Hugh Paris but also your sister, Christina, and your nephew, Jeremy."

"Your information," Smith said with a trace of contempt. "Are you so sure your information is correct?"

"I'm positive of it. Aren't you?"

"As to my sister and nephew," he said, rising, "yes. As to Hugh," he shrugged, slightly, and moved toward a window. I rose and followed him over.

"How long have you known about Christina and Jeremy?" I asked.

"Twenty years," he replied. "John Howard sought me out after they were killed and brought me the wills. I had some of my men conduct an investigation of the accident and the subsequent coroner's inquest. They established that the accident had been arranged and the inquest rigged for the purpose of a finding of simultaneous death. It wasn't difficult, Robert was inept as a murderer and left a trail of evidence that would have sent him to the gas chamber but the evidence was scattered through half a dozen police jurisdictions and the police were even more inept than he."

"But you had the evidence. Why not use it against him?"

He regarded me coolly as if deciding that I was not as bright as he'd been led to believe. "I did use it, Mr. Rios."

"Not to go to the police."

"No," he said, laying a fingertip against the windowsill. "My investigators obtained the evidence as," he smiled at me, conspiratorially, "expeditiously as possible. Their methods were not the police's methods and, consequently, my lawyers informed me that Robert would've been able to suppress enough of the evidence to weaken the case against him, perhaps fatally."

"Nonetheless," I insisted, "it was worth a try."

"You don't understand," he said, impatiently. "There were higher stakes to play."

"Something greater than justice for the dead?" I asked.

He raised an eyebrow. "I was told you had a lawyer's way with words," he said, not admiringly.

"You were talking about higher stakes."

"Yes, there was the money to think about, Christina's estate, one-half of my grandfather's fortune. It had fallen into Robert's hands. Robert was many things, most of them contemptible, but he was good with money. I had to think ahead about what would've happened to that money had Robert been removed from the picture."

"It would've gone to its rightful heirs."

"Who at that time," Smith said, "were my lunatic nephew, Nicholas, and his ten-year-old son, Hugh."

"Why couldn't you have had yourself appointed their guardian?"

"Because there was someone with a much stronger claim to that office."

"Who?"

Smith snorted. "Your client, Mr. Rios. Katherine Paris."

I said, "Ah."

"Katherine Paris," he said with recollected scorn, "a writer." It was the ultimate epithet. "She didn't know the first thing about money."

"Whereas the judge knew all about money."

"And, more importantly, I had a lever with which to control him."

"So you took the evidence that linked him to the murders and used it to blackmail him."

Smith looked out the window. A few late roses clung tenaciously to life. Perhaps they were the ones that had been named in his honor. "Yes," he said, defiantly. "Yes."

"And what did you get in return for not exposing him?"

"An agreement." He began to walk across the room. I walked with him. "At Robert's death, his entire estate was to revert to the Linden Trust, of which I am chairman. In the meantime, his affairs were controlled by my lawyers. He couldn't invest or spend a cent without my approval."

"And if he had?"

"My lawyers would've seen to it that criminal proceedings were initiated against him the second he deviated from our agreement."

"Other than your lawyers, who knew about the agreement?"

"His lawyers, of course."

Grayson, Graves and Miller — Aaron's firm. In the remote reaches of my mind something fell into place but was still too distant for me to articulate.

"So you see, the blackmail — your word, not mine — was a necessary evil."

"That seems to be your forte."

"That was cheap, Mr. Rios," he said, stopping in front of a painting that depicted the original law school.

"A moment ago you indicated that I was right about the murders of Christina and Jeremy Paris but not about Hugh's. What did you mean?"

The color, what there was of it, seeped from his face. "Robert Paris didn't have Hugh murdered," he said.

"You mean Peter Barron acted on his own?"

"No."

I was about to speak when, staring at his gaunt ancient face, the bones so prominent that I could have been addressing a skull, I realized that I was staring at Hugh's murderer.

"You," I said. "Robert Paris was your creature. He couldn't have employed an assassin with you controlling his money, unless you agreed to it."

Smith looked away.

"And of course you agreed to it. You had as much or more to

lose as Robert Paris had his earlier murders been exposed. You knew that Paris killed his wife and son and you knew that Hugh was the rightful heir to the judge's share of the Linden fortune. For twenty years you helped cover up those murders and defraud Hugh of his inheritance." I advanced toward Smith, who moved a step back. "But Hugh thought you would help him and he came to you. You leased him the house so you could keep an eye on him. He trusted you. You betrayed him."

The two guards had come up behind Smith, their hands on their guns. I stopped. Smith glanced over his shoulder and ordered them to retreat. They stepped back.

"Hugh hated his grandfather almost to the point of psychosis," Smith said, "and he knew that I was no friend of Robert's." He smiled, bitterly. "You see, Mr. Rios, I made a pact with the devil, but I could never bring myself to enjoy his company."

"That makes no difference."

"Perhaps not. Still, I encouraged Hugh's hatred of his grandfather — partly, I suppose, to deflect any suspicion from myself but also because Hugh gave vent to the hatred I felt for Robert Paris, my sister's murderer, my nephew's murderer."

"But you danced to his tune."

"Yes, I see that clearly now, but at the time, I was blind. One's own motives are always lost in mists of rationalizations. Hugh found out about the murders and expected my help in exposing his grandfather. If I refused to help him he would become suspicious of me, perhaps even guess my complicity. But I could hardly agree to help him expose Robert without also exposing myself."

"Did you tell him about your part in the cover-up?"

"Yes." Smith said.

"And he went berserk."

"Yes."

"Threatened to expose you as well."

"Yes."

"So you had him killed."

"Yes."

Smith brought his hand to his throat, as if protecting it. Suddenly, I saw the scene that had occurred between Smith and

Hugh when Smith revealed his part in the cover-up. Hugh must have responded like a madman, physically attacking his great-uncle. In a way, that might have made it easier for Smith to give the order to have Hugh killed; to regard Hugh as a madman on the verge of bringing the entire family to ruin and obloquy. Smith believed he served a legitimate purpose in having Hugh murdered, but in fact he was merely acting as Robert Paris's agent.

Smith and I had squared off, facing each other tensely across a few feet of shadowy space.

"That's not the end of the story," I said. "You had Hugh killed by Peter Barron. But where is Peter Barron?"

"Dead," the old man muttered.

"His life for Hugh's?"

"Is that so rough a measure of justice?"

"Yes, from my perspective, especially when you weigh Aaron Gold's death in the balance."

Smith shook his head. "That was unintentional. Mr. Gold worked for the firm that handled Robert's personal accounts. Shortly after Hugh's death, the partner who worked closest with Robert discovered certain documents missing that showed the extent to which I controlled all of Robert's transactions. There were also some personal papers missing, among them, Hugh's letters to Robert. The partner conducted a quiet investigation. The documents were found at Mr. Gold's home and the letters, as you know, at your apartment."

"Aaron had discovered that Paris wasn't in control of his affairs but that you were," I said, "and he reasoned that you, not Paris, were behind Hugh's death."

"Something like that," Smith said. "No one ever had an opportunity to talk to Mr. Gold."

"You saw to that," I said.

"No," Smith repeated wearily. "That was Peter Barron acting on his own. He told me he'd gone to talk to Mr. Gold, that there was a struggle and the gun went off."

"There was no struggle," I said, "Aaron was shot as he sat in an armchair getting drunk."

"I didn't believe Barron," Smith said, "since he had reasons of his own for wanting the identity of Hugh's killer secret."

"He was the trigger man."

Smith nodded. "So now you know everything," he said, "and I repeat my original question: What will it cost me to persuade you to drop the lawsuit?"

I shook my head. "It's never been a matter of money. I want an admission of guilt. I want that admission in open court and for the record. I want the law to run its course. No secret pay-offs, no cover-ups."

"My lawyers were right," Smith said, "I shouldn't have spoken to you. And yet I'm glad I did." He hunched his shoulders as if suddenly cold. "I'm not an evil man, or at least, I can still appreciate an act of human decency. I appreciate your devotion to Hugh, Mr. Rios, but you must understand that I too will have the law run its course and I will fight you with every resource to which I have access."

"I understand that," I said, "but I have two things on my side that you do not."

"What?"

"Time," I said, "and justice."

A ghostly smile played across Smith's withered lips. "Good-bye, Mr. Rios," Smith said, "and good luck."

He turned and strode the length of the gallery. The two guards fell in behind him. I waited a moment and then followed him out. I got to the top of the steps outside the museum in time to watch the silver Rolls slip away into the wood. I jogged down the steps.

I turned down the collar of my sweatshirt and spoke into the thin metal disc attached there. "He's gone," I said. "I hope you got it all down."

A moment later the white van moved into view from behind the museum. The passenger door swung open and Terry Ormes got out, followed by Sonny Patterson pushing his way out from the back of the van. Terry had insisted that I be wired for sound in the event that I was being led into a trap, so that the cops could respond. Neither of us had expected the conversation we had just heard. Patterson had signed on at the last minute, in the event that something useful was said. He walked toward me looking like a man who'd just heard an earful.

"Your little speech about time and justice," Patterson said, "ought to play real well in front of the grand jury."

"You recorded it?"

"The whole thing."

"Then there will be a grand jury."

"You bet," he said, "and if they don't come back with an indictment, I'm washing my hands of this profession."

Terry who had come up beside us, said, "Good work, Henry."

"It's not exactly how I thought it would go down."

"I'll guess you'll be amending the complaint in your lawsuit to allege Smith as a defendant," Patterson said.

I shrugged. "I'll talk to my client. She may not want to pursue the case after the grand jury concludes its business."

"You wanted it to be Robert Paris, didn't you?" Terry said.

"Yes."

"Why?"

"Smith is as much a victim as Hugh. Smith was a moderately good man who chose expediency over justice the one time it really mattered. But Robert Paris was the real thing, he was evil. I pity Smith."

Patterson looked at me disdainfully. "That old public defender mentality," he said. "People don't commit crimes, society does. You know Latin?"

I shook my head.

He said, "Durum hoc est sed ita lex scripta est — It is hard but thus the law is written."

"Where's that from?"

"The Code of Justinian, and it was engraved over the entrance of the library of my law school — which was not as big a deal as your law school here at the university, but those of us who went there were hungry in the way that justice is a hunger."

He turned from us and walked away. Terry and I looked at each other. What Patterson wanted was clear: a fair trial and a guilty verdict. My own motives were hopelessly confused — my hunger had never been as simple as Sonny's.

"Maybe," I said to Terry, "I never wanted justice but just to vent my grief about Hugh."

She shook her head. "Grief is half of justice," she said, and added, a moment later, "the other half is hope."